THE UNCHANGED

T. M. Starnes

THE UNCHANGED

T. M. Starnes

This novel is a work of fiction. Names, characters, places and incidents are either the product of the author's imagination, or, if real, used fictitiously. Any resemblance to persons living or dead is entirely coincidental.

No part of this book may be reproduced or transmitted in any form or by an electronic or mechanical means, including photocopying recording or by any information storage and retrieval system, without the express written permission of the author except for the use of brief quotations in a book review.

Cover art by:
BetiBup33 Design Studio
betibup33@gmail.com
Twitter.com/BetiBup33

Book layout by: T. M. Starnes

Copyright © 2017 T. M. Starnes
All rights reserved.
ISBN: 1548142581
ISBN-13: 978-1548142582

DEDICATION

For the everyday heroes who run to danger instead of away.

Contents

Chapter 1 1
Chapter 2 4
Chapter 3 8
Chapter 4 13
Chapter 5 16
Chapter 6 19
Chapter 7 23
Chapter 8 27
Chapter 9 34
Chapter 10 43
Chapter 11 49
Chapter 12 54
Chapter 13 58
Chapter 14 65
Chapter 15 68
Chapter 16 74
Chapter 17 80
Chapter 18 85
Chapter 19 89
Chapter 20 95
Chapter 21 102
Chapter 22 106
Chapter 23 111

ACKNOWLEDGMENTS

Thanks again to Katherine.
Thanks to the people who read my stories and enjoy them.

Chapter 1

It's hell hot. Satan's steam room hot.
So hot the devil himself would say turn down the heat. Just crazy hot and has been for weeks. Record-breaking heat. Just way too hot. Just the right kind of miserable weather to have if you're contemplating the best location to start a serial killing spree.

My latest idea for a novel involved a serial killer who traveled off the main interstates in America following old backroads. It might be a mystery, thriller, or supernatural horror. I would know by the time I finished my vacation and went back to teaching.

I like taking backroads, even when the weather is this hot, humid, oppressive and it makes you feel as if you're breathing through a damp washcloth, it's still better to take alternate routes. Trees give you shade and you get to see more of the natural world than on the interstates.

My black Wrangler rolled through the backroads of Georgia just North of I-60, on US80, heading toward a small town named Berndale to the West of Savannah, Georgia. I was taking a summer camping vacation driving from Hilton Head Island through Savannah and beyond, looking for location settings for my novel. Once, the roads had been filled with lovely green landscapes. Now, the oppressive heat wilted lawns and flowers due to the months long heat wave. I'd already considered numerous large abandoned stately homes and decrepit farms and barns. Lots of ramshackle single-wide mobile homes too. Well-kept beautiful homes held little interest for me and the plot I imagined. The photos I took were to capture the atmosphere and sense of a place. Something I typically did now after my first thriller hit Amazon and became a best seller. It helped me envision the setting for the novels.

It worked for me. If it ain't broke, don't fix it.

I drive aimlessly, taking roads that look interesting. Along US 80 and coming around a heavily wooded curve, I found a path torn through the woods on the bend appearing as if a car had driven too fast and plunged into the woods. Limbs were still falling and weeds were popping back into place. I pulled to the embankment and my suspicions were confirmed by the appearance of smoke rising from the trees.

I switched on my hazards and parked so I could be seen on both stretches of the curve, grabbed the medical kit I carried while camping, which was also necessary to the story I planned to write, and raced off into the flattened and torn brush.

The red Mazda must have had been flying! It had plunged past numerous trees and finally collided against an immovable giant. Smoke rose from the engine as I struggled to get through the underbrush. Brambles and briars grabbed and pulled at my jeans and Superman T-shirt.

"Hello!" I shouted, "Hello! Are you alright?"

When the driver's side window shattered outward I paused.

A woman with long, blood-spattered, blonde hair struggled to climb out the window, but her seat belt held her in place. She grunted and thrashed frantically.

"I'm coming, stay there! Stay there! Don't move!" I yelled.

As she struggled, the warped passenger-side door popped open and a tall, tanned man with crew-cut hair, beige slacks, and a white polo shirt kicked his way through the jammed exit, his body covered in dark discolorations.

"Hey, stay still, I have--"

Before I could finish, the man turned toward me, his eyes wild, and making a honking noise through his crushed nose as he crouched then sprang toward me.

I changed direction and fought my way back through the brambles.

"Damn! Damn! Damn!"

The briars snagged my jeans, arms, face, and hands but I kept moving.

The honking, hissing sound of my pursuer changed when he reached the same weeds I'd escaped. I didn't look back. I didn't know what was wrong with the guy but I wasn't going to let him get to me. Bath salt cannibalism wasn't that long ago.

I tripped and fell on the edge of the embankment, entangled, which made me finally look back.

The man jerked at the briars, trying to wade his way through. And he was succeeding. His exposed skin laced with scratches by the briars but he seemed not to notice it, his concentration completely on me and making that irritating honking noise.

Pulling hard enough to tear my jeans leg cuff, I rolled to my feet, aiming toward my Jeep while searching my right pocket for my keys.

The shredded man finally broke free as I slammed my door shut and started the engine. I threw it into first, popped the clutch and hit the gas. As he climbed up the bank, my tires spun and I pulled onto the road.

The nut case was chasing me!

I threw it in second.

He was gaining.

I hit third.

He began to drop back.

I glanced at the speedometer.

Twenty and he kept pace.

That's impossible.

I glanced back about to put it in fourth when his knee blew out, exploding in a gush of blood visible through his slacks, and he tumbled a good ten feet.

He rolled and bounced, I decelerated until he pushed up on his palms and, on one good foot like a rabid dog shot in the leg, trying to keep going.

I shifted and left him behind.

Chapter 2

I snatched my smartphone from its plastic cradle and dialed 911.

Nada, zip. It didn't connect.

It showed full bars, a good signal. I dialed the last person on my contact list. No answer.

My parents, my brother, my sister, my martial arts school, my agent, then random friends after that.

Nothing. Not one connected. It rang but no voicemail picked up either, which was odd.

I checked the road, pulled to the side, turned on the radio that I hardly ever used while driving since I listened to my music playlist on my smartphone. There was the whine of the emergency broadcast alert, the recorded message telling us to stay tuned, but no information followed that. It was on all stations I could pick up.

My GPS wasn't working either, I knew I was heading toward Berndale, but it said it lost the signal. I was out in the middle of nowhere I guess, maybe the GPS was intermittent.

I opened the browser on my phone and searched the internet.

The latest celebrity gossip. The latest tragedy. The latest Presidential quote.

No emergency news or phone problem announcements.

I went to my Facebook page.

No new posts...for over an hour.

My friends are pretty chatty, especially the students at my school, we posted kung fu videos all the time. Nothing new in hours. That was unusual.

I began typing.

Hey, anybody out there? I just encountered a lunatic off US 80 outside Savannah. Anyone else having trouble with their phone service? Not connecting? Where is everyone?

After ten anxious minutes, and still no response I began Googling service announcements.

The internet froze.

The internet stopped.

Either my phone is…nope, full bars…service is good…now the phone is saying no service.

"What is this?" I asked my phone, "What's going on?"

It didn't have an answer for me.

I fumbled with the dead lifeless internet, and my call list for five to ten more minutes then shifted into gear and pulled back on the road.

Five minutes later, I came to a farm. I pulled up the long driveway and drove toward the house. It was an older, white, two-story with hunter-green fake shutters and a wraparound porch. It looked like it had been there for at least fifty years. A tractor idled beside a small leaning barn to the right of the house.

I turned toward the tractor and slowed to a crawl.

My suspicious, paranoid, thriller, horror movie-stimulated mind, saved me.

An elderly man staggered sluggishly out from behind the green John Deere tractor and came toward me. A younger man, maybe his son or grandson, followed behind him, also shambling.

The younger man, wearing a t-shirt and boots, was missing an arm, his color pale, and blood squirted from the severed limb.

They were heavily bruised with purple splotches covering their exposed flesh.

Zombies? *Zombies!* Are you *kidding* me!

The younger man stumbled and fell after a few feet, tried to get up, did a one-arm push-up, collapsed and remained still as the last trickles of blood were absorbed by the earth. Zombies don't do that.

I threw it in reverse, my tires spinning, doing a quick three-point road turn into their dry withered lawn and aimed back toward the driveway.

A loud boom echoed from the house.

I know a shotgun when I hear one.

Another boom rang out.

I leaned on the horn.

I searched the farm surroundings and fields for anyone else but kept looking back toward the house.

Grandpa moved slightly faster but mostly just shambled.

The front door jerked inward, the screen door banged outward and a brunette girl wearing shorts, hiking boots and a tank top, burst out onto the porch carrying a 12-gauge shotgun in one hand and a small box in the other.

She took one look at me and ran for the Jeep.

Her wild eyes almost made me hit the gas.

"Open the door! Open the door!" she screamed.

Okay, the other two didn't speak, so I reached over and pushed the door open.

She turned, took a good stance and aimed back toward the house.

"Come on!" I yelled.

A bloodied, heavyset man with a trimmed beard erupted from the front door. She fired as he leaped off the porch coming after her.

The blast caught him in the chest and tossed him back.

She scurried into the passenger seat tossing the small box to the floor boards, scattering shotgun shells. She grabbed the door, slammed it shut, pumped down the window, and aimed back toward the house.

"Go! What are you waiting for? Go! Go!" she screamed over her shoulder.

I did as ordered, doing a double take as the heavyset man rolled over on his side and wobbled to a standing position...then began to run much faster than his bulk should have allowed.

The blast deafened me for a moment, as the girl leaned out the window and fired at the man's legs, blowing one off, leaving him face first into the front lawn. Another blast stunned me as she shot the old man, who I hadn't noticed had gotten so close to the back of the Jeep.

She pulled the shotgun back in the window as we soared down the driveway.

Failing to put on her seatbelt, her hands shaking too much, she gave up.

She began laughing hysterically, then bawling, then screamed.

My ears still rang so the screams didn't bother me that much as I grabbed her seat belt and clicked it home.

She continued screaming/crying as we pulled back onto the main road.

Chapter 3

After a few miles, avoiding other farms, she eventually settled into a quiet stare in the direction of the dashboard. I pulled off the side of the road at a home construction site and killed the engine.

She hugged herself and rocked in place.

I reached back to my rear seat and grabbed a bottle of water as I wiggled my finger in my ear to stop the ringing from the gun.

I offered her water.

She continued rocking, so I opened the bottle and offered it again.

"It's the best I have," I said.

She slowly took the bottle, continuing to stare at the dashboard.

"My name's Taylor. Taylor Walker. What's yours?" I asked.

She stared at the dashboard and didn't drink.

She looked like a typical southern American teenager.

Eighteen or nineteen, at least a few years younger than me. Long, brown hair twisted into a loose ponytail falling over her shoulder blades, sadly, covered with dirt and blood. She wore a yellow tank top, splattered with blood too, with black and beige bra straps overlapping on her shoulders. Her jeans shorts were cut-offs and frayed at the ends. Her shoes were ankle high hiking boots. Her legs and arms were bruised and scratched. One small, loop earring dangled from her left ear. Her skin was clear with no makeup. Her eyes were wide, dark brown, and red from crying. She looked five foot eight, same as me I guessed, slim, athletic, and tan.

"Do you know what's happening?" I asked.

She rocked slower.

I shrugged, "Well, I have to call you something." I tried to make her smile. "I'll call you Sally."

She didn't react.

I sighed, "Well, Sally, do you have a direction we should go? I'm not from here. My GPS isn't working and I'm not sure which way to the nearest town. I'm guessing that way," I pointed in the direction I thought Berndale lay, "although I'm not sure."

Wiggling my finger in my ear again, I opened the door to the unforgiving, blistering heat to stretch my tension-cramped legs.

Her hand shot out, holding me with a firm grip tightening around my right bicep, and dug in.

"Don't get out. Don't get out. You can't get out," she said in a voice hoarse from her continuous screaming.

I patted her hand, "I'm just standing up. I've got to stretch my legs."

Slowly, she released me.

"Please, drink some water," I asked.

She tipped the bottle to her lips as I stepped out and stomped my feet.

She made gulping sounds as she chugged it down.

I turned in a circle and stomped my feet.

"There's more in the seat behind mine."

She reached for another, her eyes not as wild, twisted off the cap and began drinking again.

"So, do you know what's going on? I can't access the internet and no one will pick up their phone. Everything's dead."

Poor choice of words as tears formed at the edges of her reddened eyes.

"I'm sorry. I meant nothing will connect. Do you know what's happening?"

She shook her head and wiped her tears, "They were my family. My grandparents and uncles and aunts and cousins and brothers and grandpa and momma and papa. I killed them. I *killed* them."

I climbed back in and wrapped my arm around her shoulder as she cried.

"I killed them. I killed them." She kept quietly repeating.

I rubbed her shoulder, "There's nothing you could do. I thought zombies weren't real but I guess anything is possible."

She shook her head and sat back, "Zombies? What do you mean 'zombies'? They weren't zombies."

Confused, I asked her what they were then.

"You didn't see the purple spots? They were pink then they turned purple when they became whatever they are." She rubbed her eyes and sipped more water.

I noticed the old man and the grandson had been bruised, they did look purple. The man who chased me on the road was too bloody to tell, I thought he was just injured from the wreck.

"I didn't really get a chance to notice."

She nodded, "My cousin Donny, he was outside, he's little, said that my cousin Aaron was standing on Jimmy and pulling too hard on his arm. Then my Aunt Lilly, she was covered in spots, came into the kitchen and started biting my mom. My dad pulled her off and she attacked him. Grandma told us to get upstairs and Uncle Bridger started fighting with my brothers Eric and Greg. Bridger was who chased me out of the house."

I let her speak but kept handing her water because her voice was so hoarse.

"Me and my little cousins, Tammy and Evan, hid in the guest room. We heard fighting and screaming downstairs. I looked out the window and Aaron was still trying to pull Jimmy's arm off. Jimmy was screaming so loud. So loud." She paused and drank.

"My grandpa came back on his tractor, he was on the back side of the farm, he loves riding his tractor. We looked out the bedroom window and we watched as he saw Aaron on Jimmy and tried to help, by that time, Aaron had torn…had…had…torn Jimmy's arm out of its socket. Aaron attacked Grandpa and then Jimmy attacked Grandpa too. Tammy and Evan were screaming that someone was coming up the stairs. I remembered grandpa kept his 12-gauge and buckshot in the closet. I told them to be quiet. I did." She shivered and cried, "I *told* them to be *quiet*."

She sniffed loudly and continued, "The closet was by the door, I was looking on the top shelf for the shells when Bridger came in. He broke the door open and it shut me in the closet and pinned the door closed. The door opened against the closet."

"Tammy and Evan…" she paused and stared out the window.

I interrupted her, "Tell me about Bridger."

She glanced at me and sipped, "Bridger heard me in the closet trying to get out after…he was done with…" she sipped, "When he pulled the closet open, I shot him. I shot him."

I remained silent.

"I thought he was dead. I came out of the closet and yelled for anyone else in the house. Tammy and Evan…they were dead…and Bridger started to get up. I ran out of the bedroom and shut the door behind me but he broke the latch. As I came down the stairs, my father was coming up…he…his face was…he tried to hurt me…so…I shot him. I shot my *daddy*!" she suddenly screamed.

I waited again until she calmed down, this time, I held her hand and she returned my squeeze.

"That's when I heard your horn. I was stepping over daddy, and Bridger broke through the door and started after me. I ran and my Aunt Lilly tried to grab me as I got to the bottom of the stairs and…I shot her." She drank some more.

"Bridger kept coming and he tripped over my dad, he fell as I came out of the house."

I stopped her, "I know the rest."

She nodded and stared out the window and drank.

I told her where I was from, that I had been camping at Hilton Head island and driving through Savannah, that I'm a writer and a martial arts teacher and why I was traveling and what happened with the man and woman back down the road. How the man was so incredibly fast and she interjected saying her Uncle Bridger never moved as fast as he did until today.

We sat in silence for a while and I offered her some candy. Candy calms me down. I have a thing for giant tootsie rolls and I don't share with just anyone, but I think she deserved at least two.

"Do you think this is happening everywhere?" She asked.

"I don't know. We're going to find out as soon as you can tell me somewhere to go."

She chewed on the melting tootsie stick, "Pull back out and go left. That's going to take you to the main road. We can see if the sheriff knows anything. They have an office on main."

"Sounds like a plan, Sally." I grinned.

She smiled for the first time, "My name's Cheyenne Stegall."

I offered my hand, "Nice to meet you, Cheyenne."

She shook my hand, I started the Jeep and turned back onto the road.

She cried quietly as I drove.

Chapter 4

We went toward Berndale and she gave me directions to turn off US80 and take a back road to Main Street. As we left the dried, browning foliage of the tall trees forming a partial canopy on the road, I slowed the Jeep as we leaned forward and considered the sky ahead of us.

Several columns of smoke rose above the trees in the distance. Otherwise, the sky remained a cloudless blue.

"Well...that's not good," I said.

"No, it's not," she agreed.

I pointed at her feet, "Why don't you reload your shotgun."

She grabbed a handful of shells and expertly started reloading.

Ahead of us, something approached on the opposite of the road.

"Is that someone on a bicycle?" Cheyenne asked.

Her eyesight was better than mine as we got closer because she saw the person running behind the bicyclist too.

"It's one of them, we gotta help," she said, rolling down her window.

The bicyclist was a young, dark-skinned, black girl with long braids tied together swinging back and forth as she pedaled. She wore a blue tank top, white shorts, and white sneakers, she stood on the ten-speed and pumped her legs as fast as she could. With one hand, she waved frantically at us.

Behind her ran a slim, tall, black man in a white muscle T-shirt, baggy jeans, and bald head. His stride was strong and repetitive, he reminded me of the man on the road.

"I'm going to pull in between them," I told Cheyenne. She nodded, her despair disappearing, and leaned partially out of the window, "I'll open my side and get her in, I think we'll have time. Shoot him if you have to."

I rolled my window down and motioned for the bicyclist to keep coming as I accelerated to intercept the man.

Slowing down, we passed her and put the Jeep between them. I put it in neutral and pulled up the parking brake. The young girl jumped off the bike as I threw open my door and yanked the driver seat forward.

"He'll kill us! He'll kill us!" she screamed running toward me and I stepped out of the way.

"Get in!"

"He's speeding up!" Cheyenne yelled.

The girl jumped in the back, crawling over my gear, and pulled her legs in.

"Go! Go!" she screamed.

I pushed the seat back and the 12-gauge fired.

BOOM!

Deaf again, I put the Jeep in first, popped the clutch and the Jeep jerked, choked and died.

BOOM!

Both women screamed but it sounded muffled.

I pressed the parking brake down, started the engine and hit the gas.

We fishtailed off the road for a moment and I ran over the girl's bike as I turned around back toward town and toward the running man.

The girl in back screamed, Cheyenne crawled back inside and stretched across me and through my window with the shotgun barrel.

The man bled, his skin looked splotchy with dark spots. Punctured with holes and his right hand was missing, he bled from his right side and part of his face lay in shredded tatters.

Cheyenne cocked the shotgun in front of my face and the shell seemed to me to eject in slow motion, ricocheting off the dashboard and falling between the seats.

"Don't fire! Sit back!" I screamed, "I can't drive! Don't shoot!"

The man collided with the Jeep and popped the side view mirror back against the car door, for a moment I felt him snag my shoulder through the open window but he lost his grip. Cheyenne climbed back onto the window sill aiming behind us. I swerved to get back on the road and she began to topple out. I reached over and grabbed her by the waistband of her shorts as she fired again.

The girl in the back covered her ears and screamed, tumbling right and left as I straightened.

"I got him!" Cheyenne yelled as I pulled her back in.

"Are you crazy! You could have fallen out!" I upshifted and took off.

She put the shotgun between her legs and buckled her seatbelt.

My ears rang, and the girl in the back had stopped screaming, staring toward our rear.

I reached out and pushed the side view mirror back, the body of the man lay in the middle of the road convulsing, I pumped the window closed and turned on the A/C.

The girl in the back leaned forward.

"Thank you! Thank you! He killed someone and chased me down the road! Everyone's gone crazy and are killing each other!"

"What? Where?" I asked.

"The whole town! The whole town is killing each other!"

Chapter 5

As she said that, I noticed a logging trail off the side of the road and turned and bumped down the access road until we couldn't be seen by traffic.

Cheyenne reloading her grandpa's shotgun as I pulled around to park in the dry dust and withered grass around the felled trees.

The girl in the backseat looked sixteen or seventeen. She was thick but muscular, she wasn't breathless from pumping furiously on her bike and was already calming. She perspired heavily, but who wasn't with this horrendous heatwave? We offered her water from my stash. The air conditioning in the Jeep blasted on full but we remained drenched. As she gulped, we waited to hear what she knew. I tried to get my ears working again, I almost berated Cheyenne for being so careless leaning out the window, but she'd been through too much already.

Cheyenne introduced the two of us to the young girl.

"I'm Janessa," the girl said, "Simpson. I live just down the road." She drank, "Is this happening everywhere?"

We shrugged, "I found Cheyenne at her grandparent's farm, her family became those things. I just found out about it when I tried to help a crashed couple back the way we came. A man and Cheyenne's uncle moved fast just like that man chasing you."

"Yeah, those are the fast ones. The slow ones creep up on you," Janessa said.

"There's different types?" Cheyenne asked.

Janessa nodded, "I've seen three so far. I was in town when people started going nuts. People did weird stuff. Walking into walls, stepping out into the middle of traffic, walking in circles. *Those* had pink spots, the violent ones had these purple spots break out on them. Big giant splotches. The people who tried to help were attacked by the people who had the splotches. The slow ones just grabbed the nearest people and…attacked them. Scratching at their eyes, biting them, strangling them," she paused, "I…even saw a lady…pull her baby's head off."

"Holy…" I said.

Cheyenne covered her mouth.

"Then a few people started swelling up. Skinny people started getting fat, like ticks, they either went after or caught people then…they threw up!" she drank some water, "They threw up on someone and deflated! It was black and purple and red. The person screamed like it was acid, and tried to wipe it off, it burned them. They ran to someone else and the stuff got on them, then they started screaming and some of *them* started to swell. I decided to get out of town and go home, but then I saw the fast ones chasing people. They're fast. The better shape they're in, the faster they are. If they catch you, they start tearing you apart. Scratching, biting, pulling you apart if they can." She drank, "That's when that guy started chasing me. He chased me out of town. I'm on my school's track team and in tenth gear and he kept up with me. He kept up with me like it was nothing. I couldn't slow down, or he would speed up."

"You go to Berndale High?" Cheyenne asked.

Janessa nodded.

"My brothers Eric and Greg go there…" she corrected herself, "…went there."

Janessa's eyes widened, "Eric Stegall? Oh, my god, I know him! My friend dated your brother Greg a year ago. Are they okay?"

Cheyenne shook her head and looked away.

Janessa didn't say a word as she leaned forward and hugged Cheyenne.

After a second or two, she did say they were great guys which made Cheyenne nod and smile.

"Are you from Berndale?" she asked me.

I shook my head, "Nope, I'm from North Carolina, a little place called Bruxton. It's on Hatteras Island."

She nodded, "What are you doing around here?"

I told her the same thing I told Cheyenne. Cheyenne was looking back down the access road as I spoke.

"I've gotta go," Cheyenne said and Janessa said she needed to too.

It took a second to realize they meant to answer nature's call.

Taking the 12-gauge, making sure the safety was on, I stood guard as they went behind fallen trees. The heat and humidity could take your breath away. Once they finished, I gave the gun back to Cheyenne and I went. By the time I came back, Janessa had already informed Cheyenne where the majority of the splotched fanatics wandered.

As we climbed back in, we heard a car zoom past the access road toward town. That meant some others hadn't changed either.

We heard the crash as we pulled onto the road.

Chapter 6

We came upon an exterminator's truck partially blocking the road. It had collided with a pickup truck crawling with the splotchy infected. The driver of the truck groggily fought an older woman crawling across the hood of his truck and over the top of a smashed black woman caught between the exterminator's truck and the pickup. The exterminator emerged from the passenger side and the slow-moving ones, the Roamers, crawled and crept toward him. He wore a white hazmat suit with his exterminator's logo and dragged a canister from the cab and put it over his shoulders by its connecting straps. He saw us coming, turned around back to the Roamers, aimed the nozzle at the nearest and released a liquid spray. The sweaty, gray-haired man then ignited the spray with something and the spray became a flame. He had made his own flamethrower with the chemicals from his business.

The man in the pickup failed in his struggles as another more determined Roamer crawled through the window and began gnawing him.

I slowed the Jeep as the exterminator's flame arced across both vehicles igniting the purple splotchy attackers.

Cheyenne rolled down her window and stretched the 12-gauge out the window but didn't crawl out.

The splotched ones began making horrible noises but didn't speed up or thrash or try to run away. They continued crawling over the dead pickup driver and advancing on the exterminator. He continued spreading his fiery arc of death.

Janessa leaned forward, "What if there's gas?"

No sooner had she said it than a small flame erupted beneath the pickup, it spread suddenly then WHOMPTH, the vehicles exploded.

In neutral, even with my foot on the brake, the Jeep skipped backward with the concussive force. Flaming body parts rained on the road, objects showered down on my convertible top. Bits of truck and car skittered back toward us. The exterminator lay ablaze several feet off the road, his legs broken, shrieking as the tank on his back exploded with a whistle and ear-shattering explosion.

We ducked beneath the dashboard and back seat but we felt the heat wave through the open passenger window as Cheyenne pumped it back closed.

When appendages stopped falling, we sat stunned for a few seconds observing the carnage around us. Several torsos still moved. Smoldering or on fire, trying to move.

Putting the Jeep in gear, we slowly rolled forward, when I pressed the brake to choose a path around the left of the double wreck, a leg rolled off my roof and toppled to the hood. Janessa screamed, Cheyenne recoiled, I tried to ignore it as I drove us around the burning hulks.

Once past the wrecks, I picked up speed and slammed on the brakes, the leg rolled off the hood and we moved forward again. I didn't want to touch it to get it off, but the brake slamming also caused purplish, black, oily blood to slide off the roof and onto the windshield. The windshield wipers didn't do a great job and there was a rank smell. At least we were going into Berndale. The A/C tried its best to cool our anxiety sweats.

Within minutes I realized there was no way I could drive with the drying blood smearing the windshield, so I told them to look for a house on either side of the road with a sprinkler or hose hanging on the front of the house as I rolled down the window, leaning out to see.

Minutes later Janessa said she saw one laying in a yard of an old single wide mobile home we just passed. I backed up and took the driveway up to the home. I tapped the horn twice and waited.

No one came to the door. Janessa kept watching behind us.

"I'm going to leave the keys in. Can either of you drive stick?"

Cheyenne nodded.

"Okay, but I need you to stand guard outside in case something comes up on me. Janessa? In the pack behind you? There's a hunting knife, my Buck knife, could you hand it to me?"

She rummaged a bit, then handed me my knife, a five and a half inch, fixed blade, wooden handled Buck knife with a brown leather sheath. I undid my belt and slipped the sheath and knife around to my left side and re-looped my belt then stepped out. I ran to the faucet as Cheyenne stepped out, holding the shotgun at her hip.

She looked like a young redneck's favorite nighttime fantasy.

The hose wasn't attached to a sprinkler but to a large hand sprayer, I told her to step back and began washing the blood and gore off the body of the Jeep. The splotchy Roamer's purple-black blood was congealing. I had to get closer then I wanted to properly spray the gunk off. Janessa remained watching our rear from the Jeeps interior as Cheyenne watched the home and the surrounding forest.

"How old are you, Taylor?" she asked.

"Twenty-three. Why?"

She shrugged, "Just wondering. You seem to be taking this better than any of us."

I didn't really want to say I was scared, but in addition to writing and the focus it takes, I reminded her that I meditated and have studied kung fu since I was sixteen, and taught it to junior students for the last two years, so I told her that instead.

She grinned, "You mentioned you taught martial arts. You know kung fu huh?"

I nodded, "I have a black belt and everything. I also do Tai Chi. You ever try it?"

She shook her head, "I've seen friends do Tai chi and Yoga in college but never really tried."

"College? Where?" I knelt concentrating on removing a piece of meat stuck in the grill, finally dislodged by concentrated water pressure.

"University of Miami. I'm going to be a cancer biologist. This was my first semester."

"Nice. I went to Columbia. A writing major. Taking a long break, though. I graduated high school when I was seventeen and went there when I turned eighteen. How old are you anyway?"

"Nineteen. I'm the youngest in my classes too."

The gore, splattered on both sides, made me nearly gag as I worked.

Janessa tapped on the window and asked if she could get out. After telling her how to push the passenger seat forward, she joined us.

The Jeep reeked. The mess was putrid. And charred.

Janessa pinched her nose shut, "Can we go to my house? I want to see if my mom is okay."

Cheyenne and I exchanged glances. I hadn't wanted to think my family was like Cheyenne's but wasn't really wanting to tell Janessa her's may be the same way.

She noticed our unspoken exchange, "I know, I know. My mom may be one of those things," She stared at the ground, "I just have to know for sure."

I shrugged, "Can we wait until we go to the Sheriff's office? We think we need to call for help or at least see if they have some firepower we can take. Cheyenne's 12-gauge is going to run out of shells sooner or later."

Janessa nodded, "If you really want guns and ammo, why not go to *General Lee's Armory* on Poplar?"

Cheyenne agreed, "Oh wow, yeah, *General Lee's*! They have everything. We could go get anything we need there."

I stopped spraying, "It's a gun store?"

They nodded.

"Sounds good to me then, let me finish with this."

A dismembered hand fell from under the front driver's side axle.

I grimaced, "This might take a few more minutes."

Janessa and Cheyenne began talking, comparing notes as I finished up.

Gunfire came from the direction of town, so someone certainly remained unchanged other than us.

Chapter 7

We crept toward town.

I shifted into four-wheel drive in case we had to make a break over uneven ground. Didn't really want to get stuck going over an embankment if a Runner came after us.

We decided to call the slow-moving ones Roamers, the fast-moving ones Runners, and the vomiting ones Volcanoes.

Roamers ruled the streets. Many infected sat in hot cars as if they didn't know how to work doors. They moved in and out of businesses with automatic doors or just wandered aimlessly. The same happened inside businesses with one-way entrances. They didn't seem to be able to figure it out.

Berndale is a small but widely spaced town. One elementary school, one middle school, and one high school. The ladies talked as we explored. Janessa ran track and was a flag girl for the band. Cheyenne had been a high school bookworm. My kind of people. They knew the back streets of the town. Cheyenne's parents lived on the outskirts on a small plot of land near her grandparents. She had an apartment in Miami. Janessa lived nearby where we found her where riding her bike or walking was the easiest way to get around.

We discussed going to the local authorities. They told me the Sheriff's office was a single story, red brick, oblong, building on Main Street in case I needed to find it on my own. There were a Sheriff and deputy or two as far as they knew. Crime barely existed in Berndale. Everyone knew everyone. Domestic violence, misdemeanors, and drunkenness or speeding were the extent of the criminal element.

We crept slowly down the street, turning right on a road to pass behind a Methodist church. I suppressed a laugh when I realized that a Methodist church sat beside a Baptist church across from a Protestant church and a Lutheran church. What the town lacked in police presence, it made up for in religious presence.

The people of Berndale were gun lovers, though. *General Lee's Armory* was a one-story building. The front of the store was emblazoned with General Robert E. Lee's profile, a Confederate flag crossed with an American flag, and paintings of guns and cannons. Thick steel bars covered all the windows and the front door. Four pickups were parked in the lot, one at an angle like it had just pulled in. The nearest Roamer was two blocks away. We pulled sideways into the lot beside the angled pickup.

"It looks like someone just got here," Cheyenne indicated the pickup.

"Anyone in it?" I asked.

She unbuckled and raised up to look into the cab.

"Nope, nobody."

"Maybe they're inside?" Janessa suggested.

"Nobody's coming out," I said.

Backing up the Jeep, leaving it running, we waited to see if anyone came out.

Cheyenne cradled her shotgun, "What should we do?"

"Maybe Roamers got them?" Janessa asked.

I scratched my chin, "We need guns. And ammo. We've got to go in."

They agreed and Cheyenne gave us a quick rundown of the ammo and weapons we would need—rifles, shotguns, pistols—and held up her almost empty box of shotgun shells as an example. She told us where to look inside and general information on rifles. I added opinions from when I occasionally researched firearms.

After I killed the engine, we armed ourselves and Cheyenne took the lead, Janessa came next, and I came last. I stayed in the rear in case we needed to hurry back to the Jeep. I would start it up as they climbed in.

Janessa and I peeked in the windows while Cheyenne kept her eye on the front door and the surrounding area. We couldn't see anything; the windows were tinted and paint obscured the insides. We advanced toward the door.

Cheyenne reached for the door, "It's got a bell that rings real loud when you open it. One of my old boyfriend's dad brought us here before he went camping once. One of those things might hear it."

She took a position on the other side of the door and motioned for Janessa to open it wide.

The electric doorbell did a loud "ding-dong" as the door opened. Cheyenne aimed inside and waited. Nothing moved. We filed in one after the other.

We kept our voices low just in case one of the Roamers wandered behind a shelf.

Once assured no Roamers waited, I spoke normally, "Okay, go find you something you feel you can use. Get your ammo and find some metal ammo boxes and set them by the door. Get at least two rifles and shotguns. I'll get our handguns."

Glancing over the displays, Cheyenne specified certain rifle shells, handguns and shotguns and what ammo would be best from the stocked shelves.

I grinned at her, "Where were you when I needed consultation on weapons for my stories?"

We followed her down the rows. Janessa picked three metal ammo boxes by the front counter and Cheyenne moved toward the rifle and shotgun sections and I went behind the counter of the handgun section. I grabbed a canvas bag for other things we may need.

Someone already partially ransacked the cases. Smashed glass lay within the display cases. Probably someone seeking protection too. Several weapons were missing from behind the counter and several handguns too. I grabbed two Glocks that I thought the women could handle. In my research for a previously unsold story, I learned that if your wrists weren't strong, the bigger, longer-barreled handguns could fly out of a weak grip. So, I avoided them. Glocks were better and came with a standard clip. I grabbed a SIG Sauer 1911 for my own use. I liked the way it looked. Cheyenne took down shotguns and rifles and placed them on the floor, testing their weight and test cocking them. One with a lever action. She examined boxes of shells behind the counter too, reading them for compatibility I suppose.

I found a box of ear plugs and happily tossed them into my bag.

My eyes lit up when I noticed the word "The Colt" on a little slip of paper inside an undamaged case and the pistol it offered.

I grew up watching old reruns of Westerns. The Colt .45 was my dream gun. While I sided typically with the Indians over the cowboys because I studied factual Western history and knew that the white man really did do the natives wrong, the Colt .45 was and will always be my dream gun. Mostly because the weapon just looked cool. "The Colt" was actually a Colt lookalike from Uberti. A single-action six-shooter, with a brass 5.5" barrel and brown walnut handle. It looked like it was fresh out of a Western.

Glancing at Cheyenne's serious face as she picked out her haul, and Janessa's rapt attention on ammo, I sighed.

Sometimes you have to just be a kid.

I knelt and found ammo for the Colt, I loaded its 6 cylinders, grabbed several boxes of ammo for it, found a matching holster, a cool, badass Western-looking one and tossed the holster into my bag. I set the loaded Colt down on the counter as I went back to looking for what we really needed.

When I stood, I smiled at Cheyenne sitting on the floor behind the counter engrossed in reading the specs on a rifle with a mounted scope. She sighted down the aisle away from me and checked the lever action. It looked like a Winchester. Janessa was in the aisle in front of me, picking boxed shells carefully off the top shelf, setting them into the metal boxes, and then test lifting them. They were heavy judging by her tensed muscles.

I froze when Janessa bent over at the waist to place more shells in her box, and two armed men, one older and one younger, admired, with leering expressions, her legs and her white running shorts stretching across her rear end. They stood in front of an open door to an office that we ignored, assuming it was storage.

The older man whistled and grinned, "Well, what do we have *here*?"

Chapter 8

I'm not blind. I know that Janessa and Cheyenne are beautiful women. I'd been trying to ignore that fact concerning Cheyenne while we were in the situation we were in. Cheyenne is closer to my age so I don't feel bad admitting she's attractive in a spectacular way. But Janessa is just a kid. She's the shapelier of the two, well-endowed with full rounded hips. Her chest stretched the limits of her sports bra and she's physically well beyond her years of actual maturity. She's athletic and yes, quite attractive, but still, she's a kid.

The older man, a white man, appeared to be in his late fifties with a three-day-old beard, balding, with wisps of black and gray hair and was dressed in camo. He leered at her backside as she quickly stood up. Two handguns were pushed into the front of his pants and he cradled a 12-guage in his left arm. A canvas bag sat on the floor to the left of him, stacked money and guns filled it to the top.

The second man was a younger, slimmer version of him, with a military style crew cut and armed with a camouflaged hunting rifle.

Janessa straightened and spun in surprise at the sound of the older man's voice. She glanced back at me and both men's attention shifted to me. The young man's rifle slipped into a two-handed grip and the older man's shotgun lowered from a resting carry and angled toward the floor but in my general direction.

The older man examined Janessa from foot to head as she slowly stepped backward.

"Hello, Mister Stanton. Hi, Jeff," Janessa said, continuing to step backward.

"You know her, son?" the older man asked.

Jeff nodded, "She's on the track team. She's a Junior."

His father made a lecherous face, "Ain't nothin' junior about her. I can see why she's on the track team. Girl, you got a hell of a pair of legs."

I didn't glance at Cheyenne. Peripherally, I saw her moving and carefully loading whatever weapon she had in her hand. The

Colt sat on the counter by my hands. It was obscured from the other men's sight by a sale standee.

"Who are you, mister?" Jeff asked me, "You with her?"

"Hi there, I'm Taylor," I waved my left hand at them in a small salute, "I guess you're doing the same as us. People have gone nuts out there, time to load up and protect yourself."

The older man kept leering at Janessa who walked backward until she bumped up against the counter in front of me to my left. Something made her uncomfortable with these two men. I felt it was more than the comments.

The older man's gaze left Janessa's chest and looked me over.

"How do you know her, hippie Superman?" he asked.

It took me a moment to understand what he asked. I wore my blue shirt with the Superman symbol but I didn't understand the hippie comment. My brown hair covered my ears but it was hardly as long as a hippie's. I guess compared to his it could be considered long.

I smiled, "We met while she was being chased by one of those fast purple people."

He pursed his lips and nodded noncommittally, his gaze casually moving back to Janessa's chest. She crossed her arms over her breasts and glanced back at me, fear evident in her eyes.

"Aw, no reason to be shy," the older man said, "If you didn't want us to look at them watermelons you wouldn't wear that."

Janessa's loose shirt covered her sports bra, only the straps barely showing on her shoulders. Nothing suggestive at all. I wasn't liking where this was going.

"You're not bad looking for a colored girl, even with them braids. Kinda dark, though."

Colored? Do people even use that term anymore?

Jeff moved further into the aisle with his dad. His dad took a step toward Janessa.

"Janessa?" I said, "Come back here with me."

The older man's eyes locked with mine, "Nah, she ain't gonna do that."

Janessa started to move sideways.

His shotgun slowly raised toward me, "I *said* you ain't gonna do that."

Janessa froze.

I judged how quickly I could grab the Colt and fire if I ducked behind the glass.

It wasn't good, and glass doesn't usually stop bullets.

Cheyenne moved behind the counter but I kept my gaze on the father.

"Look, guys," I smiled pleasantly, "What's going on out there is pretty bad, we all need to work together. We just want to get some weapons and get out of here. No harm, no foul."

The old man's mouth shifted into a sneer, "Jeff?"

"Yeah?" His son said.

"Keep your gun on him. I don't like thieves."

As Jeff's rifle raised to his shoulder, I lifted my left hand in surrender, "Hold on now, we didn't know you owned the place. I've got money, not a problem."

"They don't own the place," Janessa softly whispered, her arms still crossing her chest.

I glanced at her and back at the men.

The older man grinned, "Well, technically we do now. Bobby Lee was one of them things. We had to kill 'im, and we were here first. So, by rights, we own it," his smile grew into a leer directed at Janessa, "...and everything in it."

This was not looking good.

"Look we don't want any trouble-" I said.

"Ain't gonna be none..." he shrugged, "...as long as she shows us what's under that boulder holder."

Janessa started to cry.

"Dude, she's a kid," I said.

His weapon pointed at me again, "I don't care. I want to see 'em, and I want to see 'em now. And maybe a whole lot more. *Dude.*" He grinned the greasiest, most malevolent grin I'd ever seen outside of a bad B-flick.

Janessa slowly shook her head back and forth.

"Oh, you're gonna do it, Janessa," Jeff said from behind his dad, his barrel aimed at me, "Then you can show us other stuff. Maybe in the back."

"Or right here," his father corrected.

Janessa's shoulders began to shake and she started murmuring "please" repeatedly.

The older man slowly stepped toward her, "Oh, come on now, we know you give it up to all them young bucks. It's time to see what a real man is like."

Janessa tried to step to her left and he adjusted his direction to follow. A few more steps and he would see the Colt on the counter behind the sign.

"Don't make me chase you, girl. I don't got time for that. Now get over here and take off that top."

Damn it to hell.

I inched toward the Colt.

Cheyenne suddenly stood from behind her hiding place.

She cocked the lever action of her rifle as she aimed it at the younger man.

"Hey, Jeff," she said.

Jeff turned toward her, just his head visible above the shelving, a breath after that, her rifle blast took off the top of his head.

The older man screamed as his son's skull exploded. His shotgun rose as I grabbed the Colt with my right hand, leaned forward, and shoved Janessa to the left out of the way as he fired.

The shelfing took most of his blast as Cheyenne fired wildly and ducked back down.

My first shot hit him in the right shoulder, staggering him, he grunted and dropped his shotgun.

Janessa scrambled behind the counter as I fired again and missed.

He drew one of the pistols from his waistband with his left hand and Cheyenne's rifle fired and missed.

I fired, hitting him in the chest. He staggered back and tried to lift the handgun. I fired twice more. Two more hits, in the chest once more and the neck, and he toppled backward.

He hit the ground with a thud and coughed blood.

I kept the Colt on him as Cheyenne hurried beside me.

The older man relaxed and his blood began pooling with the river from his dead son.

My hands shook. Below the counter, Janessa had her arm wrapped around my left leg in a death clench. Cheyenne shot the dead man once more in the chest, screaming at him, saying that people like him should be the monsters and not her family. She dropped her rifle on the counter, turned, and threw up to our right, barely missing my ammo box and bag collection.

I screamed in frustration.

A primal scream at the stupidity of the two men.

I screamed again for myself because I just killed someone.

Cheyenne finished her vomiting. Janessa slowly stood and looked over the counter. The Colt and my empty palm pressed into the glass counter in defeat.

"They were bad people," Janessa murmured.

Cheyenne turned around and agreed with her, "That was Jeff Stanton, right? From the football team?"

Janessa nodded.

Cheyenne looked at me as she wiped her mouth, "He raped a girl from school a year ago. His dad was friends with the judge. They went hunting together. The judge had most of her testimony thrown out. Jeff got off with six months' probation. The girl moved away, I heard she tried to commit suicide several times."

"She was black too," Janessa added, "Jeff was into black girls. He always creeped on me and my friends at school."

I couldn't think of anything to say so I hugged Janessa and pulled Cheyenne close too.

"Thank you," Janessa told us.

We gathered our gear, stepping into the blood around the men to retrieve the box of ammo Janessa left on the floor and transferred the dry boxes to another container. The boxes of ammo were so heavy we divided them between us. Janessa bagged the rifle Cheyenne used, a Winchester lever-actioned 150th commemorative issue, and a Remington 870 tactical 12-gauge with front and rear pistol grips, draping the straps over her arm. Cheyenne wielded her grandfather's reloaded 12-gauge in one hand while holding the strap attached to a long canvas bag that carried a Remington 700 bolt action rifle over her left shoulder and a Ruger .22 carbine rifle. I carried most the ammo, found us some holsters with belt loops for their Glocks and tossed them into our bags. We would find belts later. We were mostly silent, avoiding mentioning the dead men on the floor, as we gathered to go back outside, my hiking boots leaving footprints behind us.

The canvas bag of money the Stanton's set down with stacks of hundreds rested on top beckoned to me. I picked it up and looped it onto my left forearm.

We hurried to the Jeep and piled in. The afternoon heat continued to be even more oppressive and humid. Clouds dotted the sky but there were no storm clouds in sight. Roamers slowly progressed down the street toward us from either direction attracted by our movement.

"Where to now? Janessa's house?" I asked, starting the engine.

Janessa nodded, "Go two streets back, take a left and go straight, I'll tell you where to turn."

Cheyenne set loose shells on the dashboard and rolled down the window.

"After that, we need to get to the sheriff's office. There might be someone there. We can contact the authorities." She smacked her lips, "I hope you have a spare toothbrush at home."

Janessa snickered, we laughed and I turned the Jeep around. Our first real laugh since this started. A welcome relief. We didn't talk about the Stantons as I pulled onto Poplar Street in front of *General Lee's*.

Through Cheyenne's open window we heard a roar ending in an echo bouncing off the flat, walled surfaces around us.

"What the hell was that?" I asked.

Cheyenne pumped up the window as we weaved between two Roamers, an older white woman and a once-tanned twenty-something guy, the purple spots covering them. The diseased woman was close enough to catch Cheyenne's gaze; purple lines crisscrossed where the whites of her eyes had been.

"Don't know, don't want to find out," Cheyenne said, turning to watch behind us with Janessa until Janessa began sorting ammo and exchanging firearms with Cheyenne to load and pass back.

Cheyenne knew guns.

As I hit fifth gear and turned off Poplar, another mysterious roar rose then receded into the distance behind us.

Chapter 9

Janessa's house was further than she made it sound.

She must have some strong legs and lots of endurance to walk that distance to school.

Berndale city limits stretched wide across the wooded landscape. Along the way to Janessa's house, we encountered numerous cars with people collapsed against the dashboards and cars stopped on the side of the road, the engines still running. Once or twice as we passed a vehicle, purple spotted arms rubbed against the derelict cars windows.

I didn't want to imagine how hot it must be inside those enclosed cars with the dead or even with the infected. Or how it must smell. Our air conditioner ran full blast but the roof and windows remained hot to the touch.

Several people lay on the ground or on porches as we passed through neighborhoods. Janessa told us that as she peddled through town, when whatever happened had happened, some people with the pinkish spots dropped and lay still. The ones with purple spots collapsed, thrashed, or squirmed, as unaffected people moved to help their fallen friends and family. Janessa stopped to help someone but then people started screaming when she looked back up from the pink spot covered person at her feet, several Roamers dragged people down and a jogger or two ran after others, tackling them, beating and biting their victims.

Thinking, like most people who grew up with zombie movies, that it was a zombie outbreak of some kind, she fled, and soon after, was chased, until we intercepted her and her pursuer.

We passed a neighborhood with a smoke cloud, possibly a house fire, rising from deeper in the community.

"Take your next left," Janessa said from the back seat as she handed Cheyenne a loaded pistol, barrel first.

Cheyenne freaked out, slapping the barrel away from her.

"Careful! Don't hand me a loaded gun aimed at my face without the safety on! What's wrong with you?" she grabbed the pistol from her.

Janessa pulled her hand back.

In the rear-view mirror, Janessa looked close to tears.

"Easy, Cheyenne, she didn't mean to."

She spun on Janessa, "You could have killed me! Don't you know how to handle a gun?"

"Cheyenne?" I cautioned, I knew it was tension and trauma from our recent events.

Janessa slowly shook her head.

"Wait," Cheyenne softened immediately, "you really *don't* know how to handle a gun?"

Janessa shook her head as I took the left turn.

Cheyenne studied her for a second, "Janessa. I'm sorry. Have you ever shot a gun before?"

She shook her head.

Cheyenne nodded and then looked at me, "Other than back there, have you?"

I nodded, "Mostly a .22 rifle and pistol. A double-barreled 12-gauge. And a Glock once or twice."

She grinned, "Farmer's kid?"

I shook my head, "Farmer's grandkid. We shot targets on his farm."

She grinned at that. She reached back and took Janessa's hand.

"I'm sorry I snapped, we're going to have to teach you really fast. Hand me that Ruger .22 rifle behind you. Yes, that one. Until we can show you how to aim with a pistol, let's go with rifles." Janessa handed Cheyenne the rifle. Cheyenne pointed at the safety and told her how to turn it on and off, "Aim down the barrel, don't worry about the sight right now, shoot from the hip if things get close. But if you do use the sight, you line up the back sight even with the front sight. It'll take practice. It'll have a kick so hold on. I don't want to start you with a shotgun, it'll knock you on your butt."

She reached back for another rifle, "This Remington is bolt actioned so you'll have to eject the shell each time before you fire. It holds five rounds. Keep count, reload often. I think it will be the easiest to start with."

Janessa nodded, "Thank you."

Cheyenne nodded and gave her a box of ammo for the Remington, "Load her up."

After realizing Janessa had no idea how to, Cheyenne showed her how to load the first two shells, ejected one using the bolt action, then handed them back to her. Cheyenne then showed her how to load the Ruger .22. She suggested Janessa start practice with the Ruger and work her way up to the Remington.

Janessa looked up and touched my shoulder, "The red brick house with blue shutters on the right just ahead."

Janessa's house was a ranch style home. The yard was immaculate. There was a two-car carport with no cars beneath. She explained that her mother usually road with a friend since their car had a slipping gear and it was in the shop.

"What does your mom do?" I asked crawling up the driveway.

"She's a Nurse Practitioner. She's helping out at a retirement home, today is her day off."

"And your dad?"

Janessa's expression dropped, "He died in Afghanistan when I was six."

Cheyenne and I shared our condolences as the Jeep came to a halt.

No one came to the door.

Janessa gripped the backs of our seats.

I glanced back at her in the mirror, "Um…let me go check. Maybe she's not here. Maybe her friend came and got her."

Janessa barely raised her voice, "She was here when I left after lunch."

"Brothers?" Cheyenne asked, "Sisters?"

Janessa shook her head, "Just me."

I started to get out then exchanged a glance with Cheyenne, we had the same thought.

"Janessa…" I began.

"I know," Janessa wiped her eyes and sniffed, "She might be one of those things."

Cheyenne handed me the Remington tactical shotgun, "We may have to…"

She nodded at Cheyenne, "I know."

I checked the area and stepped out, "Watch my back."

Janessa patted her .22 in response and Cheyenne started to get out of the Jeep.

"Where are you going?"

Cheyenne frowned and gave me a strange look, "I'm standing guard."

I nodded, cradled my weapon, and went toward the front door, stepping up the short steps.

Once at the front of the house, I listened at the window by the door, I glanced back at Cheyenne's watchful gaze and the hopeful eyes of the teenager in the back seat.

Shaking my head, indicating I heard nothing from inside, I rang the doorbell.

No sounds from inside.

I knocked. Nothing. I banged. Nothing.

"She says to check the back deck!" Cheyenne yelled.

I nodded and moved around the right side of the house. Cheyenne tracked me and stepped outward and toward the house so she could see the woods around us, the Jeep, the front and side of the house and me.

Stepping away from the brick wall, the heat waves from the bricks adding to the misery of the rest of the day, I stepped around to a wonderland of colors.

Janessa's backyard was a botanical paradise.

A half-acre of foliage. Green, reds, yellows, and oranges bloomed in multiple groupings. Their water bill must be huge. Her mother certainly has a green thumb. Enraptured by the beautiful landscape behind the house, I nearly fell over when I looked to my left toward a lovely wooden raised deck and who could only be Janessa's mom staring at me from five feet away.

When I jumped back, Cheyenne called my name.

I waved at her that I was alright as Janessa's mom continued staring.

With her dark skin, the pink spots looked white. She lay across the deck railing, her arms over the railing holding her body upright. On the ground beneath her hands lay an empty coffee mug.

Her eyes were clouded over and flies swirled around her body and face as I stepped closer.

I looked back at Cheyenne, dropped my gaze and shook my head, pointing toward Janessa's mom.

Cheyenne dropped her gaze, nodded, and waited. When she glanced toward the Jeep, out of my angle of view, I heard Janessa's anguished scream.

She knew what I'd found.

I raised my hand for Cheyenne to go help her as I banged on the side of the house for any other surprises, just in case.

Cheyenne must have opened the Jeep door because Janessa's screams increased in volume.

A tarp lay on the ground in front of the deck. As I went to grab it, the wind picked up and I could smell the deceased lady. It was horrific. I placed my shotgun on the railing, grabbed the tarp, saw some work gloves, put them on, and hurried up onto the deck. I put the tarp down, checked her mom for any signs of life just in case, then, braving the dark horde of flies disturbed in their meal, I pried her stiffened body away from the railing and down onto the tarp. Footsteps hurried around the house. Cheyenne called out to Janessa just as Janessa came around the corner as I folded the tarp over her mom. Janessa fell to her knees and screamed over her mother's covered body.

Cheyenne came around the corner, looked at me, knelt beside Janessa as Janessa cried on her shoulder and hugged Cheyenne for support.

Once Janessa calmed, she asked me to take her mother into her beautiful garden and lay her in the middle of the Asian lilies she pointed out were her mom's favorites. Cheyenne finally broke down and started crying too as I carried Janessa's mother away.

I thought about my family. My mom and dad, my brother, my sister and her husband and their baby, my nephew. I worried, but I wanted to have hope. If I believed they were dead, or worse, one of these infected creatures, then I wouldn't, couldn't, imagine what I would do. I thought of my brother teaching college classes, big know-it-all, and my sister and brother-in-law fighting over the latest color of their baby's room. She was a perfectionist but she did have style.

My mom and dad I didn't want to even consider. My dad kayaking, my mother wanting to hike. Teasing each other about their favorite TV shows and why the others were completely without any appeal.

I shook my head to clear the thoughts as I came back to the porch, removed the gloves and set them on the blistering hot glass table on the deck. Flies lingered, searching for their missing meal, and I waved them out of the way to retrieve my shotgun.

Janessa found the back door unlocked and Cheyenne waited for me while scanning the area around the house, and we went inside together.

Blissful air conditioning!

As beautiful as the exterior of the house, the interior confirmed Janessa's mom had a fantastic interior sense of taste also.

A relaxing home décor. Medical journals and books were placed here and there. Over the fireplace mantel sat a boxed, tri-folded flag and above it the picture of a good-looking Sergeant in desert camouflage gear. Hundreds of photos covered the walls. Janessa as a little girl with her father, mom, and dad together, Janessa with sports teams, older people I assumed were grandparents, just a plethora of memories.

Cheyenne hurried through the living room, through the kitchen to the front door, she scanned the front of the house for movement. She came back into the living room and plopped onto an overstuffed brown couch followed by a relaxed sigh as she stretched out her arms and wiggled into the comfy couch.

Janessa moved into the kitchen, blew her nose, washed her hands, opened the refrigerator and brought back a six pack of blue Gatorade for us and we greedily tore off one apiece and drank.

"Can you see what the news says?" Janessa asked, pointing at the coffee table in front of Cheyenne.

Cheyenne leaned forward, grabbed the remote in front of her and aimed it at a thirty-inch flat screened TV behind me.

I stepped to the side.

Static.

No EBS.

No news.

Not anything on any channel.

Just static and seconds later, text saying 'no signal found'.

Cheyenne turned off the TV and dropped the remote, plopping back again.

"Do you think this is a terrorist attack?" Janessa asked.

Cheyenne huffed, "Pretty stupid attack if it affects everyone. Unless it's a suicide attack, then they could care less."

I shrugged, "Who knows? Global warming? The end of days?"

Janessa shushed me, "Don't even joke about that."

Cheyenne gulped down her Gatorade, "Do you have a shower I could use?"

Janessa nodded slowly, still in shock I thought, "Sure," She looked at Cheyenne's sweat-stained clothes, her own, and then at mine, "We could all take a quick bath."

"I'm fine with that," I said.

We followed her further into the house.

The rooms fit in with the rest of the house.

We looked in at Janessa's room.

Pictures of athletes adorned the walls. I recognized Gabby Douglas' Olympic pictures. Serena Williams. Laila Ali. Of course, Flo-Jo running along a track. Several black male singers I didn't recognize, Eminem I did. I was surprised to see Mae C. Jemison in her astronaut garb, the first African-American woman in space. Beside her, I recognized Nichelle Nichols dressed as Uhura in Star Trek. Books lay everywhere.

I smiled. Beauty, brains, and an athlete. Well done, mom and dad.

She showed us to the bathroom and shower. Ugh. A girly girl bathroom.

Candles, oils, flowers, lotions, African American hair products, feminine things. Ugh.

She told us to go first, but we felt Janessa needed to relax the most with the shock of the loss of her mother, and she moved numbly toward the bathroom.

Cheyenne would be next, then me.

Janessa offered to give Cheyenne fresh clothes, but everything fit too baggy or too small. Where Janessa was short, curved and abundantly endowed, Cheyenne was taller, slim, and smaller chested. Cheyenne declined and said she would find something later.

I offered to get her a shirt from the camping gear stowed in the back of my Jeep. She readily agreed, and we returned to the withering heat outside and I rummaged through the back as Cheyenne stood guard.

I grabbed a bright blue T-shirt for myself. I waved several shirts at Cheyenne until she picked a green workout tank top. I offered her fresh socks and picked a pair for myself and fresh underwear. Cheyenne stopped me and asked if I had another pair of boxers. I did and she accepted the final clean pair I owned.

Back inside, as Janessa began her shower, I made sandwiches for all of us from what I found in the fridge.

Cheyenne and I talked as we ate.

She didn't want to go back to her grandfather's farm for anything. Only a weeks' worth of clothes remained anyway that she brought from college. She knew of a store in town she could get some clothes but mine would do for now. She didn't want to see what remained of her family either. She said she felt like she was going to break any moment. She asked me about my family and I told her about holding out hope, but I tried to be realistic too.

Janessa reappeared, handing Cheyenne soft, thick, white towels and off Cheyenne went, then Janessa and I talked.

Janessa wore a fresh pair of powder blue running shorts, a loose red t-shirt with the Berndale high school logo across the front and running shoes. Her long braids were damp and she let them dry naturally because she was just too tired to do anything with them.

She mentioned her mom, then her dad, then her mom again and started to cry but steeled herself, blew her nose and dropped the subject.

She told me more about the town and the infected and the first moments of the plague.

Cars crashing, screams, gunfire, and more screams. People running for their lives, monsters moving everywhere. As she ate, she stared out the back window at the garden. I checked to make sure she couldn't see her mom from her viewpoint and she couldn't.

"Taylor? What are we going to do if the whole world is like this?" she asked.

Remembering rousing speeches from several novels and from real life that I loved, I couldn't think of a single answer. Except one.

"We go on," I shrugged.

She looked at me before biting into her sandwich, "That's it?"

I shrugged again sipping my Gatorade, "What else can we do? Give up?"

"I guess so," She bit into her sandwich.

"How are you doing?" I asked.

She knew what I meant, "I'm…scared. I'm sad. I feel sick to my stomach. But my mom would have wanted me to remember her, and keep…" she smiled, "…moving forward."

"Sounds like a plan," I nodded and winked.

Cheyenne returned, patting her long brown hair dry, wearing her frayed shorts, my green tank top tied in a knot at her chest forming a midriff-baring shirt, her flat belly exposed, my blue boxers rolled above and over the waistband of her shorts, moisture glistening on her skin, down her legs, down her cleavage and her neck.

"God, that's so much better," she said, "Thank you for the toothbrush too. There's another for you, Taylor."

She glanced up at me when I didn't respond.

I realized I was staring.

Janessa snickered.

"Well?" One of Cheyenne's eyebrows rose as she looked at me, "You gonna shower or not?"

I nodded, set my drink down, and ignored Janessa's grin as I walked by her and she told me where to find the towels.

Girlish laughter followed me as Cheyenne laughed and said "Boys."

Chapter 10

Oh, that was just what I needed!

Clean teeth!

I dressed and put away soiled towels and bundled my clothing to return to my bags.

We asked if Janessa wanted to stay home until we returned from the sheriff's office but she told us she would feel safer with us. We gathered drinks and food to munch on for energy even though it was a short ride back into downtown Berndale. We shifted my camping gear around in the back of the Jeep, positioned the weaponry for easier access and stacked the ammo in an order we all understood and could get to if we needed. We covered the money and put it in the bottom of the pile. I put on the holster with the Colt and slipped the Buck knife already looped through my belt onto the holster belt

Loud rapid gunfire came from the direction of town.

I searched the cloudless blue sky as I listened, then it dawned on me.

"Guys, have you seen or heard any planes go by?"

Janessa and Cheyenne looked up.

Cheyenne frowned, "No, come to think of it. One of the flight paths out of Savannah comes right over Berndale this time of day."

Janessa agreed, "It drives my mom crazy."

Janessa realized what she'd said and looked sad for a moment.

The rapid fire came from town again.

We looked at each other.

"Military?" I asked.

They shrugged.

"Is there a reserve unit nearby?"

They looked at each other, Cheyenne frowned, "No. There's a VFW. The nearest reserve station is thirty minutes toward Savannah."

The rapid shots were followed by three concussive explosions.

Without another word, the three of us climbed into the Jeep, I did a three-point turn and pulled back out to go back into Berndale.

***

We rolled the windows down as we neared the edge of town.

Cheyenne leaned out the window to listen as she gave directions for which way to turn to go toward the sounds of combat.

It might have been counterproductive to head toward a firefight but it meant military or survivors at least.

We reached the rear of commercial buildings, turned right, and ran right into a collected group of Roamers as we turned the corner.

I put the Jeep into reverse as the thirty-odd Roamers turned around.

"No! Stop! There're two Runners behind us!" Janessa yelled, looking out the back window.

Glancing in the side mirror, two Runners, an older man in a torn business suit, and a younger man with bloodstained legs wearing nothing but jockeys, were in full charge.

Cheyenne unbuckled and leaned out the window.

"Hold onto her!" I yelled.

Janessa grabbed Cheyenne's waist as I whipped the Jeep around.

BOOM!

Deaf again. Where's those ear plugs I grabbed?

BOOM!

"Hold still!" Cheyenne screamed.

I shifted into first and gunned the engine. The tires spun and she screamed and grabbed the window.

The Roamers increased their speed but were infinitely slower than the oncoming Runners.

BOOM!

I may be mostly deaf at the moment but I could certainly hear Cheyenne shouting curses.

BOOM!

I aimed us toward the Runners, the Roamers blocked the other way.

BOOM!

The pantsless Runner rocketed backward and fell, twitching to the ground.

"It's clear on the right! Go right! That alley right there! Right there!" Cheyenne screamed smacking the top of the Jeep, "Janessa, give me more ammo!"

Janessa grabbed three shells rolling around in the passenger seat and shoved them into Cheyenne's free hand.

Cheyenne screamed obscenities at the Runners as she reloaded.

BOOM!

I whipped toward the right and down the alley, halfway through, an obese Roamer wobbled on the right side. A bearded man whose shirt and jeans squeezed his girth relatively compactly into what appeared to be grossly undersized apparel, turned toward us.

BOOM!

Janessa looked out the windshield, saw the Roamer ahead and screamed, "Get in! Get in! Cheyenne get in!"

Cheyenne was paying attention to the Runner behind us and screamed at Janessa to stop pulling on her.

Then I remembered what Janessa had said about fat Roamers.

The Volcanos.

I reached over and wrapped my arms behind Cheyenne's knees and dragged her in.

She was fairly light so it wasn't that hard but she nearly dropped her grandpa's shotgun as her elbow banged against the windowsill and she demanded to know what was going on. Janessa shoved Cheyenne against the dashboard and cranked the window up just as the Volcano turned around at the sound of our engine.

It was disgusting.

The window sealed as the Volcano let loose and Janessa bent over Cheyenne in a protective posture, covering her with her body even with the window closed.

Vile, purple, black, clotted bits of meat, sinew, and entrails erupted from the Volcano along the right side of the Jeep. We could smell the rotting stench through the convertible roof. Cheyenne bumped the stick shift as we flew past the deflating spewing Volcano, the engine's RPM almost redlined before I could shove her thigh off the shifter.

The Runner was almost on us.

I shifted into third, nearly choked it, downshifted to second, then Cheyenne's thigh bumped the gear shift again as Janessa crawled off her, the RPM's soaring again.

"Get off the shift!" I screamed.

I threw it into second as she pulled her legs up to her chest to give me room.

The Jeep lurched as we acquired our fourth passenger.

Janessa screamed as the purple-splotched businessman clawed at the rear plastic window, one arm wrapped around the spare tire and his feet planted against the rear bumper.

Janessa seized the nearest weapon, the Remington bolt action, and used the butt of the weapon to bludgeon the Runner trying to scratch through the plastic rear window.

In the rear-view mirror, the deadly end of the barrel pointed at the back of my head.

I ducked and weaved as I drove, avoiding the barrel and screaming "It's loaded! The gun's loaded! The gun's loaded!"

She paused for a second realizing what I was saying as I spun the Jeep out of the alley taking a sharp right turn, throwing everyone to the left. I threw up my arm to hold Cheyenne off the shift, then realized I was heading right at an abandoned car and swerved to the left to avoid it and everything flew toward the right. Another abandoned car, too damn close, made me swerve right. The Jeep shook as the Runner dislodged and I shifted gears to get away.

The Runner scrambled to its feet and returned to its pursuit. The fallen dead littered the street every few yards, sizzling in the sun with legions of flies having a field day, and Roamers turned toward our commotion, changing their direction. Swarms of flies burst into flight as we passed, on the dead and the changed Berndale citizens alike. We bounced over a speed bump that had been a person lying in the street and Janessa and Cheyenne bounced a few inches toward the ceiling.

Cheyenne started to pump the window down to return to her onslaught but Janessa grabbed her arm.

"No! No! It's like acid! That stuff on the Jeep is like acid!"

Cheyenne realized that her side of the Jeep and the window was covered with dark purple goo and screamed in frustration. She dumped shells into the floorboard and her lap and finished reloaded the shotgun.

"Go left! Go left!" Janessa yelled, "It's the main street!"

I took a left and the Runner remained in hot pursuit. I couldn't accelerate fast enough to lose it with all the obstacles in the street. An obese woman with close-cropped blue, disheveled hair, spewed eruptions on our right as we passed but we avoided contact.

"Right!" Janessa screamed.

I turned onto the street and collided with two Roamers, a teenager and a four-foot-tall little girl on the corner throwing the teenager through a store window and the little girl on the hood of a car.

"He's still coming!" Cheyenne yelled.

We drove on the stretch of road that was US 80. It bisected the center of town. Cars, mangled dead, black clouds of flies, Roamers, and Volcanos dotted the cityscape. I zig-zagged through the stationary vehicles. We smelled the reek of hot eviscerated humans lying on the sizzling tarmac. Splotchy infected turned toward us and began their slow marching.

"No!" Janessa yelled, "Another Runner!"

The side mirror reflected a second Runner, a woman in a tennis outfit, keeping pace with our pursuer, virtually shoulder to shoulder.

"Move! Move!" Cheyenne said as she crawled into the back, "I can shoot them out the back!"

"Watch the gearshift!" I screamed watching her legs moving toward the shift.

When I looked back up, a desert camouflaged Humvee barreled straight at us, a soldier poking out the top motioning frantically for me to go right.

"Shit! Look out!" I yelled, pushing Cheyenne down between the seats with my hand on her lower back and butt.

Janessa must have seen the Humvee coming toward us and let out a bloodcurdling scream.

We passed so close to each other I could see the Steelers football logo on the baseball cap of the gray bearded driver and I could see the color of his eyes.

They were blue.

And he was laughing.

I looked in the side mirror as they passed.

The Humvee collided with the two Runners. The soldier sticking out the top ducked down just before impact. The businessman exploded along the left side of the vehicle, his chest bursting open, while the tennis player cartwheeled into the air, one leg partially detached and landed hard enough to break her neck.

The Humvee tires squealed and skipped to a halt.

I inched to a stop, angling left. The soldier reappeared at the top of the Humvee and waved with both hands for us to follow them. Then he manned the mounted, scary-looking machine gun on top of the Humvee and aimed it back toward us.

I hesitated, unsure if he was going to shoot us.

The driver opened his door and leaned out. His beard hung down his chest and rested on an ample gut. He shouted something at me.

I rolled down the window to hear.

"Get yer ass in gear, boy! You don't want to be on this road right now! Follow us! Move it! Move it!" Then he let out a wild laugh, slammed the door, the tires spun and the Humvee took off. The soldier on top sighted over the Jeep and behind us toward something we couldn't see.

The monstrous roar we heard earlier echoed from that direction.

I whipped the steering wheel to the left and accelerated after them.

The roar emanated again and I quick-shifted to catch up with the Humvee weaving through the town and the purple diseased.

Chapter 11

We raced after the Humvee as it made a generally straight line, avoiding Roamers but often not. The driver drove like a maniac. The soldier on top, rocking and whipping back and forth with the motion of the vehicle, kept the mounted machine gun aimed over our head and behind, swiveling the weapon right and left as they passed side streets.

"What's he looking for?" Cheyenne asked.

Janessa looked behind us and Cheyenne joined her, "I don't see anything. Anything new I mean."

I kept my eye on the Humvee, swerving where he swerved and going where he went. I realized we cut down side streets and doubled back once or twice before we returned to US 80. Once back on 80, the Humvee accelerated and so did I. We aimed for the stretch of road with the churches, whipped onto a road between churches, flew past cemeteries on either side, bounced roughly across three raised speed bumps, then turned abruptly into a funeral home's rear entrance.

The soldier directed us toward a covered garage area attached to the funeral home on their right, the maniac driver fishtailed the Humvee to a stop, threw it into reverse and backed up into the covered garage. The soldier continued aiming over their hood back the way we came. We pulled in beside them. The driver pressed a controller on the dashboard of his vehicle and a side rolling gate, on our left as we looked out of the garage, separated us from the parking lot and hid us. The soldier disappeared within the Humvee.

Our driver's side doors faced one another and the maniac Santa Claus-looking driver stepped out.

"Good going there, son! You kept up!" he grabbed a rifle from within the cab.

I stepped out and Cheyenne and Janessa leaned over to see him.

When he turned back he saw them.

"Holy..." he leaned back to give the passenger room to look out, "Pete? We have *ladies.*"

An older black man in the passenger seat leaned over like the women did, he wore a Vietnam veteran baseball cap and the left side of his face was slack, "There is a God." he slurred as he spoke.

The soldier leaned forward from the back, saw the women, smiled and waved.

Needless to say, I was immediately cautious due to our earlier experience with the Stantons.

The heavy-set man took off his Steelers football team cap, "Ladies, forgive us, but Pete, Jerry and I were beginning to think only men…adult men…weren't affected by this purple disease. Thank goodness that ain't so."

He noticed their reluctance and my tense posture.

He put his hat back on, "Aw, don't worry son, as handsome as I am, my days of being attractive to the opposite sex are long over." He winked, "Whether I want them to be or not." He motioned with his thumb into the Humvee at the soldier, "Jerry you might need to worry about, but Pete?" The older black man saluted with his right hand against his cap brim, "He's too ugly to even worry about."

"I got sex appeal," Pete grinned," That counts for a lot."

The maniac laughed and extended his hand to me, "Name's Roger. Hospital Corpsman First Class Roger Coltrane, USN, retired. That's Sergeant Pete Williams, retired, and my buddy Carl's nephew, Lance Corporal Jerry Underwood, also retired, they're Gunners. Current surviving members of the Berndale VFW in good standing."

I introduced myself, then Cheyenne and Janessa as Pete climbed out and made his way slowly around the front of the Humvee. His left side was limp and slack, possibly from a stroke. He dragged his left foot, partially cradled his left arm and the left side of his face remained motionless. He wore a Harley biker T-shirt, black pants, and adjusted his Vietnam Veteran baseball cap with his good hand. Pete and Roger appeared to be in their late sixties or early seventies.

Pete heard Janessa introduce herself using her last name as he came around to shake my hand, "Janessa *Simpson*? You related to Milly Simpson?"

Janessa leaned further out over the driver's seat.

"Yes, sir. Do you know my mom?"

He nudged Roger, "Milly's girl. Dang, she's as pretty as her mom," Roger agreed, "We sure do, young lady, she comes out to our retirement home. Come on out and let's take a look at you."

Janessa pushed the seat forward and began climbing out the driver's side as Cheyenne went to open her door.

Furious banging on the side of the Humvee stopped us all.

Jerry slapped the side of the Humvee, shaking his head and pointing at Cheyenne and the top of the Jeep.

"What's that?" Roger said and looked into the interior of the Jeep, "Whoa. Hold on there sweetheart, that gunk'll take your arm off. Crawl on out this side, Jerry'll wash it off, that's upchucker guts. You don't want it on you."

As Janessa stepped out, Cheyenne climbed out over the seat as I held the door open for her.

"Cat got his tongue?" Cheyenne grinned at Jerry as she stepped out.

Jerry appeared older than me in his mid to late twenties, his desert camo accentuated the deep tan covering his arms and shoulder. He removed the helmet he wore when manning his weapon and had replaced it with a soft desert camo cap. His uniform sleeves were rolled up and his left arm had faint scars tracing up to his neck. On his neck, chin, and temple were thicker scars. Even with the scars, he was a decent looking guy.

Roger patted Jerry's shoulder, "No, ma'am, Jerry can't talk. An Afghani IED took his voice box and most of his tongue. They had to reconstruct his whole jaw."

Cheyenne apologized immediately.

Jerry smiled, nodded and waved to ignore it.

"Oh, don't worry, Jerry's fine. He wasn't much of a talker before he deployed." He grinned and wiggled his eyebrows at her, "And he's *single*."

Cheyenne blushed as Jerry pulled back inside the Humvee and exited the vehicle on the other side.

"Let's go on inside," Roger waved, directing us toward the garage door connected to the building, "We found a few other people. Where are you folk's from?"

I told him my origins and Roger recognized Cheyenne's grandfather's name.

"Oh, yeah, I used to bail hay with him when we were little, he was a few classes ahead of me at school." He glanced at her, "Is he...?"

Cheyenne shook her head, "My whole family is gone. They're those things now."

Pete asked about Janessa's mom and she told them what we found. Pete gave her a hug and Roger gave his condolences.

Roger hugged Cheyenne with his free arm, "I'm sorry sweethearts. Y'all ain't alone. Come on in. Grab your guns, though, you need to carry firepower all the time now."

Jerry came around the back of the Humvee and extended an odd-looking gun to Pete. A grenade launcher that looked like a shotgun with sights and a large tube for a barrel, with three grenade cartridges attached to the stock by a belt with three of six slots empty. Pete could hold it one handed if he rested it against his good shoulder.

Pete took it with his working hand, "There's my little Thumper, you'll get that sucker next time, baby," He kissed the launcher.

Janessa stared at the launcher as we trailed behind Pete into the building, "You use that? On what?"

Pete gave her a lopsided grin, "It's for shooting that big ugly. I shot one of those Tanks. Missed, but still, it hurt her. Blew her off her feet. We saw her getting up as we drove off."

"Tanks?" I asked.

Roger nodded then realized we didn't know what they were talking about.

"The big one. The all muscled up one?" he noticed our blank stares, "That roaring thing back there? Thing's like something out of a video game."

"The roaring?" Cheyenne asked, "We heard the roar but didn't see anything."

Pete nodded, "That's her. You're lucky you didn't come across her. Eight feet tall, even Jerry's M60 mostly just slowed her down. She absorbed half of his shots and kept coming. Strong as a tank, ugly as a mule, all ridged and bumpy and spiky. Skin looked like purple rock," He kissed his launcher, "But you'll get her, won't you girl? She looks like a woman Roger used to date, come to think of it."

Roger grinned and shoved him, "Ya'll ain't seen her yet?" he asked.

We shook our heads, "We've just seen the Roamers, the one's that throw up, and the ones that are really fast. You're saying that someone…transformed into some sort of monster. I mean a monster different than those other things?" I asked.

Roger whistled, "Then you're in for a surprise when you see the Tank. There's another type we call a booby-trap. It lays in wait, you think it's one of the people that those purple people killed till you're right on it and bam! Up it jumps and got ya!"

Jerry opened the interior garage door to the funeral home's interior and we found ourselves looking down the barrels of six guns and the wide-eyed fear of at least nine kids.

Chapter 12

Jerry raised his free hand and motioned for them to lower their weapons.

Two men in their thirties and nine middle and elementary school-aged children waited behind a barricade at the end of the hall.

The two men, wearing sweat-stained summer clothing, motioned for the kids to step back so they could move the barricade of tables and an empty overturned coffins. Two girls, one in a sundress, and the other in shorts and a t-shirt carried camouflaged hunting rifles that were as tall as they were. Three tall, gangly boys, who looked like brothers, held pistols. A third girl, around nine years old, held onto the younger kids.

We introduced ourselves as we sighed in appreciation at the cool interior of the Funeral parlor.

Roger and his friends had found the survivors wandering the streets and running from the diseased during multiple excursions. The two men were from out of town, just passing through, caught in the traffic wrecks. The kids were from Berndale. The three boys were, indeed, brothers. The youngest girl had been playing in a park with the boys when they had watched their parents change and begin attacking people. They hid and the girl found the smaller ones just as the Humvee drove by, searching the park for children.

Roger, Pete, and Jerry were at the Berndale local chapter of the VFW enjoying the air conditioning and TV until some of them collapsed, convulsed, splotched purple, then attacked their friends. Jerry's uncle Carl attacked Jerry, but Roger pulled him off which made the uncle attack Roger and Jerry had to kill him. Pete was battling a nursing assistant until Roger and Jerry came to his aid. Roger joked that Pete owed him poker money and he wasn't getting out of paying him back that easy.

Twenty dollars is twenty dollars after all.

After the beginning of the outbreak, Roger, Pete, and Jerry ran into the owner of the funeral home out on the street. The mortician had been retrieving an old woman who passed from the oppressive heat at their retirement community a block from the

VFW where most of the vets lived. The mortician told them that the funeral home had reinforced doors, windows and a garage where they could hide. The homes and businesses around the VFW were going the way of the purple-splotched masses. Jerry found the keys belonging to the Humvee on display on a pink-spotted, dead, soldier who had been part of the Veterans appreciation day display in front of the VFW. The three friends confiscated the weapons brought with the reserve unit setting up for the appreciation day. The reserve volunteers had left to get breakfast just before the outbreak. Jerry volunteered to be part of the appreciation day group and wore his uniform and would have displayed and explained, as best he could, how to use the M60 top-mounted weapon when they would eventually relocate to a nearby shooting range later in the day.

Berndale citizens enjoyed their firepower and those who served.

On their way to the funeral home, the three of them and the mortician encountered the monster woman they called the "Tank." The Tank was rugged. The undertaker and the hearse didn't survive the creatures attack and the rest fought the Tank until they evaded her pursuit. They lost her for a time as they tried to find other survivors. They circled back and found the keys on the dead undertaker before going to the funeral home. On their second trip, they found the youngest girl and the littlest ones. On their third, they found the two men and made a run to *General Lee's Armory* too. They made no mention of the dead father and son. They brought the weapons back to their improvised base and set out for their fourth run. The Tank found them as they sought food and drinks.

The Tank was semi-intelligent they said. It tracked them, they doubled back several times and zig-zagged through town, but the thing found them. It shrugged off the M60 machine gun to their shock. They explained that, when they shot the Tank, the shells either were absorbed, or they formed spiny ridges as they passed through her body. Pete's grenade shelling stunned it enough that they could make their getaway. That's when they ran into us, and we followed them back here.

Jerry tapped one of the other men and pointed at two walkie-talkies lying on a table.

The younger of the two men shook his head, "Still nothing but static."

Roger frowned, "Dang. You would think either the military or the police would get through."

"We were heading to the sheriff's office," I asked, "Did you already go there?"

Pete huffed, "Yeah, the first place we thought of. It's deserted inside. It's a small force, only three deputies and a secretary. All the cars were gone and the secretary wasn't around. We grabbed one of their radios and tried to call for help but all we got back was static. Same thing with the military."

"Ain't a damn thing workin'," Roger sighed.

Cheyenne grabbed a water bottle and drank, "So you haven't seen anything on TV or the internet? Regular Radio? Not even on the Emergency broadcast system?"

Everyone shook their heads, "Nope, right when it started at the VFW?" Pete shrugged, "We were watching TV. No news breaks. Just happened. After a bit, we realized no stations were working. The EBS did come on for a minute or so just before the screens went dead station by station but no information at all. Just that whine."

Jerry excused himself as he stepped between us, pointed at the garage and made a hissing sound as he pointed with his finger.

Roger nodded, "He's gonna wash off the gunk from our transportation," He smiled at Cheyenne, "He wouldn't mind some help."

Jerry rolled his eyes, blushed, and made an OK gesture and pointed for us all to stay there.

"Are there any hospitals nearby?" I asked, "Maybe we could get some information from them?"

Roger shook his head, "We got mostly animal hospitals here and nothing else past Patterson till you get to Savannah. We were planning to do a search and rescue for other folk, then head toward the big city. We're a small town and spread out, but we got close to three thousand folks hear-a-bouts." He took off his cap and brushed back his sweaty gray hair, "We could use some help."

I glanced at Cheyenne and Janessa. They nodded.

The two other men declined since they had no working vehicles and someone had to stay with the children.

Roger nodded, "That's good, you two know the building now, you need to stay and protect our base." He patted the older girls and boys on the back, "Y'all got to be our sentries again. We're heading out, and coming back as soon as we can. We gotta find us a bigger ride to take us all but one that'll maneuver. Can y'all hold the fort till then?"

The men and the children nodded.

"Taylor, you and the ladies come with us. We got a map in the back of the Humvee, we're going to a dealership where they sell SUV's. It's just down the road a piece. We can pick up one or two and come back."

Jerry burst through the garage door and beckoned us to the front of the funeral home.

"What's got into that boy?" Pete asked hurrying after him.

When we reached the front of the building, Jerry pointed at his ears and then outside.

We couldn't hear it from the back of the building but we could from the front.

We opened a window and it became louder and clearer.

We heard a fire engine siren and someone yelling for help over a loud speaker.

Chapter 13

Roger went into action, "All a y'all, get your gear. Come on, you three." He turned us around.

He gave directions as we moved back to the garage.

"That's the fire station's siren and loudspeaker." He grabbed his rifle and a pocketful of shells, "It's in a bad area. We drove through there. Place crawlin' with those Booby-trap things, buncha Runners and lots of cars blocking the road. Not to mention the slow poke walkers. Buncha casualties lining the streets too."

Pete grabbed his grenade launcher and Jerry returned Cheyenne's grandpa's shotgun and handed Janessa the Glock that she'd brought from the Jeep.

Jerry rushed past us, grabbing three stacked metal ammo boxes from beside the garage door entrance and disappeared into the garage.

"Listen, folks," Roger stopped us, "I saw inside the back of your Jeep. You got firepower. That's good. But understand somethin'," he looked at Pete for confirmation, "You see that Tank? You see it coming near us? You got a clear shot? You open fire. You keep firing, you don't stop till you run out of ammo on *every* one of your guns. If she goes down, you keep firing. She trips? You keep firing. Pete blasts her with a grenade, you keep firing until y'all are so far from her you can't see her no more. Y'all understand?"

Pete agreed with his orders and we nodded that we understood.

"She's gonna scare the crap outta ya when you first see her. You open fire. *Don't* let her get near the Jeep. She *will* flip y'all. You understand me, Taylor?"

I nodded.

"Let's roll," he said as we hurried to our vehicles.

The garage floor was slick and smelled horrible. Jerry had washed the Jeep clean and much of the diseased flesh off the front of the Humvee. I went to the back of the Jeep and unzipped one side of the convertible rear window so Janessa could fire out the back through a small gap on either side window. I explained to

Janessa what I was doing and that she could shoot out the sides, then hurried to the driver's seat.

"The towns-folk ain't human no more," Roger yelled as he waited for Pete and Jerry, "They'll kill ya. Kill 'em first, y'hear?"

We nodded.

He pressed the control for the garage door and it slid open as Jerry, wearing his helmet again, popped up to man the M60.

The Humvee engine roared to life and Roger let loose with maniacal laughter as the back wheels spun and the Humvee leaped out of the garage like a tiger roaring from a patch of jungle growth.

I backed the Jeep out to the left and took off after them.

"Guys? I'm really, really scared," Janessa said from the back seat.

Cheyenne looked back at her and took her hand, I smiled at her in the rearview mirror.

"Don't be," I told her, "We have Cheyenne to protect us."

Cheyenne laughed and raised her grandfather's 12-gauge, "Just keep the shells coming."

"Do you mind if I pray?" Janessa asked. We frowned at her, "No, not at all, why would we mind?"

She turned around and placed her hands on the makeshift armory we had in the back seat. She began praying for the weapons to work, the ammo to not misfire, prayed for the Jeep to work, prayed for Cheyenne, prayed for me, prayed for herself and those we'd lost and were lost among the diseased. She asked the Lord to watch over us as we saved people and to watch over the souls of the infected that were trying to kill us.

We wove through cars and the dead, the purple splotched diseased, and the remains of what the Humvee had aggressively moved out of their way.

The fire engine sirens grew louder.

"Runner," Cheyenne said, pointing out her window, pacing alongside the Humvee, she rolled the window down, and heat and stench blew in as she aimed at a barefoot, teenage boy running ahead of us after the Humvee and fired.

I kept forgetting to find my ear plugs.

The Runner flew through a shop window as it was hit.

Jerry waved at us from his turret and gave Cheyenne a thumb up.

She gave him one back as she rolled up the window.

The sirens grew louder. I couldn't understand why the Roamers were thicker in this part of town. There were just as many cars as the rest of town, it *was* US80, but still, they seemed to be congregating here. Or possibly moving through to another location.

The Humvee slowed and Roger stuck out his arm and pointed for us to take a left.

As we turned, we saw why he changed direction.

A dense roadblock of wrecked vehicles stopped our forward progress, multiple Roamers, maybe thirty, turned toward us stuck amongst the wrecks. We followed the Humvee into a side street. One Runner, a long-haired Hispanic woman, leaped up on the hood of a car and came after us, hurt, but keeping a good pace.

"Janessa?" Cheyenne asked, "You want her?"

Janessa thought about it for a few moments.

"Never mind, I'll do it." Cheyenne started to roll down the window.

"No. No, I'll do it." Janessa said, picking up the Ruger .22 rifle, and pointed the barrel out through the rear window zipper.

"Rest it against your shoulder." Cheyenne coached as I drove, "Let her come closer."

I cautioned them, "We're about to take a turn."

BANG.

Where. Are. My. Ear. Plugs!

"Try again." Cheyenne calmly instructed.

Janessa rubbed her right shoulder but aimed again, lying back down on my camping gear.

"Just-" Cheyenne said.

BANG.

In my side mirror, the Runner fell forward and rolled to a stop.

"Good shot." Cheyenne praised.

When Janessa turned around, tears stained her face and she hugged herself and massaged her shoulder. Her long braids fell across her face and shoulder, Cheyenne reached back and held her hand.

We turned to the right and took a back street.

"I killed someone," Janessa said, "I killed a person."

Cheyenne consoled her, "No, Janessa, no. They're not normal people anymore. They're…" she thought about it, "…they're diseased. Rabid. They'll kill us. They'll kill you."

Janessa nodded slowly, wiping at her tears.

"It's necessary," I added.

Cheyenne turned back around, looking out her window, and scratched at the side of her face with her left hand, after a second, I realized it wasn't just an itch.

I reached over and pat her on the leg to reassure her.

She glanced down at my hand, stopped scratching her face and covered my hand with hers. then slid her hand beneath mine and held my hand. She tried her best not to cry, but her soft gasps behind her loose hair covering her face betrayed her.

She let go when I had to down shift.

Keeping my mind on the mission, and not on the two traumatized women with me, I hurried after the Humvee. I'm sure I was traumatized too, but how would I know? I was on the inside looking out. I could see *their* pain, but I couldn't recognize my own.

Jerry suddenly opened fire in the direction we were going.

The M60 spat shells that bounced off the Jeep's roof, hood, and windshield.

Janessa and Cheyenne picked up their weapons again.

Ten Runners, four on the left and six on the right, ran toward the Humvee and Jerry filled them with holes. Two Volcanoes erupted from the sidewalks but were too far back to hit either the Humvee or the Jeep. Cheyenne pumped down the window and shot one of the Runners as we passed. Janessa fired out the back window but didn't hit anything so Cheyenne finished a wounded Runner that Jerry's M60 hadn't stopped.

We turned right and headed back toward US80.

The siren was much louder now, and we could hear a woman's pleading voice between the alternating siren blasts: "Help us! Is anyone out there? Please. Please. Help us!"

We turned left back onto US80. Behind us lay the opposite side of the roadblock we avoided.

The fire station was on our right. An engine sat in the driveway with sirens blaring and lights flashing. The woman's voice came from the speakers attached to the station.

Roamers milled around the fire engine. A purpled, dirty, blond teenaged boy Runner climbed over the top of the engine, hurrying back and forth along the top like a caged animal.

Jerry released a short burst and the Runner toppled backward. He then opened fire on the Roamers below. Once they were killed, they pulled up and stopped in front of the fire engine so they could see down each stretch of road. I pulled in on their right and parked between them and the front of the station.

The woman's voice stopped and a panicky, tanned, blonde haired woman wearing a white flowered sundress peered out one of the windows.

Roger leaned out of the Humvee, "Can you see to her? We'll cover you! See how many there are!"

Pulling up the parking brake and putting the Jeep in neutral, I jumped out and ran toward the front door. Cheyenne, without prompting, stepped out of the Jeep and stood guard. Two dead firemen lay between the building and the Jeep.

The side door entrance of the station jerked inward and I nearly drew my pistol but it was the woman and she carried a limp, unmoving, pink-splotched girl.

"Help us! Help us!" she cried running toward me.

The tiny little girl, blonde like her mother, wearing a similar sundress, jiggled as her mother carried her toward me.

"My daughter's sick! She's sick! We need an ambulance!"

I slowed, realizing the little girl had to be dead, then stumbled backward as one of the firemen to her left suddenly sprang to his feet and launched himself at the woman and the dead, diseased child.

"Taylor!" Cheyenne screamed.

"Booby-trap!" Pete yelled from the Humvee.

When I scrambled back to my feet, trying to draw my pistol, Cheyenne and Pete screamed at me to get down. But the fireman was going to kill the woman. She dropped her child to defend herself against the infected man.

Time slowed for me, but it happened quickly.

By the time I had drawn my Colt and aimed, the fireman had already bitten into the woman's neck and cheek. Her neck muscles and half of her face, including her ear, came free with a geyser of blood ejecting from the woman's throat. Pete was screaming. Cheyenne was screaming. Janessa was screaming.

The Colt bucked in my hand.

The fireman twisted away from the woman with a bullet in his side, his attention turned toward me as he released the bleeding woman and she crumpled to the pavement.

My Colt bucked again and the fireman's head whipped back and he fell backward.

I shot the other fireman lying on the ground beside that one in the head, just in case, as I rushed to the woman.

She held the side of her face, her teeth exposed through the cheek, and choked on her own blood.

I knelt, and she grabbed my shirt, trying to speak.

I leaned forward and everything continued moving in slow motion. She spat blood and tried to speak again. When she couldn't, she pointed with bloodied fingers at her daughter beside her.

I nodded, and I think I told her I would take care of her.

She relaxed and died.I stared at her for a moment.

Suddenly, two hands slid under my armpits and pulled me to my feet.

"...coming! We have to go! We have to go!" Cheyenne screamed as time sped back up.

Jerry's M60 was firing around the front of the engine, and he was *not* stopping. Pete screamed at Cheyenne as she pulled me toward the Jeep.

"Get him in! We gotta go!"

"Taylor? Are you okay! Can you drive?" I staggered into a run and she let me go, *"Can you drive?"* she screamed more forcefully.

I slapped myself, "Get in! I'm okay! I'm okay!"

Running around the front of the Jeep, holstering the Colt, I raised my hands over my head to protect myself from the hot rainfall of shells expended from the M60.

Cheyenne jumped into the passenger seat while yelling "Let's go! Let's go!"

Roger was revving his engine in front of us and the backup lights came on.

Jerry continued firing, the shells creating a metallic rainbow.

The view ahead of us was obscured by the wailing fire engine, we had stopped in the middle making a 'T' with the engine and the Jeep.

I put the Jeep in reverse and backed up so the Humvee could retreat.

As I turned the wheel sharply to the left, the Humvee started backing up, and the M60 stopped firing, but only to reload.

Pete yelled back at us, "Back the way we came! Move! Move!"

Then a roar echoed off the fire station and our windows.

The Tank was coming.

Chapter 14

Fear gripped me with the roar's ferocity and volume.

I skipped first gear and put it in second and the Jeep leaped forward.

Aiming toward the side street we'd exited when we pulled onto US80, I was concentrating on avoiding the dead, the diseased, and the abandoned vehicles in front of us, but Janessa's gasp of surprise made me check the mirror.

"Cheyenne! Cheyenne! Look!" she yelled.

Cheyenne turned around and looked back between the front seats, "Oh my *God!*"

I glanced at the side mirrors and the rear-view mirror at what went on behind us.

The Humvee kept close, right on our bumper, moving left and right as Jerry continued firing up top. Pete used his good arm to stack ammo boxes so Jerry could reach them.

I saw the Tank running behind them only in side to side glimpses.

It was…

It was…

It was female, but you wouldn't know it except for the breasts.

It was misshapen, purple, humpbacked, with a malformed face and skull. Brown patches of hair dotted one side of her head, long when she was unchanged but now short due to the transformation in height and bulk. She stood a towering eight feet tall.

The Tank wasn't as fast as the Runners, but she was quick for her size. Runners ran from her. Roamers turned, hid, or squatted as she passed. Volcanoes moved from her path.

Her height, her muscles, so many muscles, rippled as she pursued the Humvee. Humpbacked, weighing hundreds of pounds, with her right shoulder higher than her left, but her right arm was larger than her left. She was nude, probably having grown out of her clothing as she transformed. Her left breast was lower and smaller than her right but they both were gigantic and moved like loose, slow, pendulums as she ran. She had a twisted grotesque face and her right eye was lower and larger than the left.

You could feel her footfalls. With a slack jaw, the black syrup which made up her lifeblood dripped freely down her neck. Her skin, while purple, was also pink. The pink parts looked like scabs, and spiky, pink protrusions poked out of her back, legs, and arms like a porcupine. The spikes appeared solid and strong. Overall, she looked rocky.

The M60's barrage only slowed her down. Perforated, her body oozed goo for a moment then healed. If the bullets passed through her, the spikes grew as a result as they exited, sometimes longer, sometimes shorter.

As she passed the wailing fire engine, she shoved it out of the way so she could pass between it and a car stopped in the middle of the road. Then she brought her right fist down like a hammer on the cab of the fire engine and the sirens died. She crushed the cab halfway into the interior, the glass of the windshields blowing outward. She turned back to the insect bites from the Humvee and resumed her pursuit.

I pressed on the accelerator, the engine revved, and I remembered to shift.

Cheyenne and Janessa screamed to go faster. The Tank was getting closer to the Humvee. I spun us to the right and the Jeep teetered on two wheels before I regained control. We flew down the side alley, the M60 firing in short bursts as they turned in behind us. The machine gun chatter stopped momentarily as we traveled straight. Seconds later, sporadic chatter from the gun started again.

We turned left, I downshifted, upshifted, then accelerated.

We were in a stretch where we could come two abreast and the Humvee roared up beside us. Pete yelled at me and I pumped the window down to hear, decreasing my speed only slightly.

He yelled between machine gun fired, "Split up! It….us…Go…we'll…meet…home base! Go…to…UV…get…back…luck! Get transport!"

I understood, nodded, and they dropped back.

"Which way to the dealership they mentioned?" I yelled over the machine chatter.

Janessa shook her head, "I don't know!"

Cheyenne slapped the dashboard, "I do! Go right, two streets down!"

I increased my speed, avoided a few Roamers, turned right where she pointed and seconds into the turn, a Roamer blocked our path in the middle of the road.

Cheyenne ducked, Janessa leaned down behind her, and I ducked just as we collided with the purple bald man.

If he had been heavier, he would have shattered the windshield, instead, we struck him, he hit the glass, causing a four-inch-long crack, rolled over the convertible top and fell behind us. I picked up the pace and kept going.

Cheyenne gave directions to go straight along a clear stretch of wooded road and I floored the pedal, shifting into sixth. In the side mirror, the Humvee flew past our turn and seconds later the Tank hurried after them.

The machine gun chatter grew fainter the further we went. We drove down back and side streets with sparse houses eventually becoming none. We made another right and came back onto a little-used, potholed road and Cheyenne said to go straight and we would come up on the back side of the SUV dealership.

Our breathing slowed and we drank from our supply.

The machinegun chatter died in the distance along with the Tank's roaring.

Chapter 15

Unsure if we were going in the right direction, I asked if Cheyenne was certain she knew where we were going.

She grinned, "Yes, I am," she winked at Janessa, "Lots of backroads to go parking and drink beer along this road."

Janessa grinned back at her as she tied her long braids into a thick knot, "I wouldn't know anything about that," but her grin meant she might.

Cheyenne laughed, "You will," her smile slowly disappeared, "Or would have."

An uncomfortable silence followed for a moment until I saw the tall dealership sign poking out above the tree line.

Before Cheyenne could guide me, I nodded, "I see it."

We pulled into the back lot of the dealership through an open-gated fence surrounding the property. Employees' cars were parked in the rear. Several rolled up garage doors with various car maintenance signs describing what service each bay provided. Heat waves undulated over the pavement and off the metallic surfaces of the vehicles in the back and front of the building. It was a small dealership to service a small town and the adjoining town further down the road. The lot was filled with family cars, trucks, and SUV's.

At the front of the building, we discovered at least one female Roamer eyeing us from the wall of windows at the entrance. We drove completely around the parking lot searching not only for the purple diseased but also SUVs that could carry multiple people. The lot was a combination of new and pre-owned cars. We found no diseased but we did find two new, and potentially perfect, Suburbans. One white, one red and a black family van.

We parked the Jeep beside them, kept a look out as we got out to inspect them.

The doors were unlocked and the heat inside was like a furnace even with the passenger and driver windows partly open. Cheyenne crawled into the driver's seat of the red vehicle as she handed me her shotgun and Janessa crawled into the passenger side.

"It looks like we can get at least five passengers in this one," Janessa said, "with some room in the back for one or two more. All the survivors if they pack themselves in."

Cheyenne nodded, "Think you could handle it?"

Janessa stared at her, "Me? Drive this?" she inspected the driver's console, "I haven't been driving that long, not by myself. Just six months. This is the biggest thing I've seen. My mom's car is small, this is huge."

Cheyenne turned to me, "What do you think?"

I shrugged, "It's automatic, of course I can."

She smiled, "No. I mean, do you think she'll be able to handle it?"

Janessa's worried expression told me she was unsure.

I shook my head, "We need someone experienced at the wheel."

She nodded, "Well. Then it looks like we take this one. I guess I'm driving. We can go back and get the survivors, take them back here, load up the kids or go back and get them and then…" she thought for a moment, "…then…Savannah, I guess, like Roger said."

"You don't sound so sure."

"Do you think it's a good plan?" she asked me.

I shrugged, "It's Savannah, or somewhere else," I thought for a moment, "Although…if post-apocalyptic stories are accurate, the greater the density of people, the greater the chance of danger."

She pursed her lips, "That's what I was thinking too."

Janessa leaned forward to look at me standing outside, "I was thinking it too."

I drummed my finger on the hot open door, "Well. One thing at a time. Let's save the survivors, and then figure out a place to go."

They agreed and Cheyenne glanced back at my Jeep, "Do you want to upgrade?"

I looked at my black beauty.

Dents, peeling paint discolored from Volcano vomit, the cracked windshield, and purple-black blood-goo stuck to the exterior and convertible top. She'd looked much better this morning.

I looked over at the more modern, newer model Jeeps grouped together to the side in the Pre-owned lot and then back at mine.

"Nah. I'm loyal. I won't give her up till she quits on me, or she's so used up that I'd have to put her down myself."

Cheyenne grinned.

I shrugged, "She's gotten us this far, she's paid for, and I've had her for a long time and for lots of miles."

"Good outlook you have there," she said.

"Huh?"

"Not giving up on *her* until she quits on you."

Janessa grinned too.

I thought some womanly mind melding was going on there that I didn't understand.

"Yeah, well," I pointed toward the building, "We better go find the keys. Do you want to check any others? How about this van?" I pointed at the black van beside us.

We inspected the black van but the women preferred the red suburban.

I was outvoted.

We hurried through the lot on foot, but except for pickups that would offer no protection at all, the Suburban and van had to be it. The other vehicles were too small and couldn't carry that many at once with supplies.

Cheyenne suggested that Janessa bring the Remington bolt action rifle to get rid of the lone, well-dressed but bloodied middle-aged woman pacing against the front of the building's windows. We could see two people lying on the floor inside. We agreed to shoot them before we got too close in case they were Booby-trap springing ones.

The diseased woman followed us to the entrance and I put my foot against the door to stop her from exiting, Cheyenne stopped the adjoining door. The diseased woman bumped against the door and slowly smeared her purple gunk-blood over both windows trying to reach us. A pen stuck out of her chest.

Cheyenne tapped the window in front of the purple woman, "At least they're not smart enough to open or close doors. I noticed that with some of them trapped inside houses."

The woman's eyes were wide, bulging, the whites covered with purpled veins.

"Do you think...they can be helped?" Janessa asked.

I shrugged, "If this *is* going on everywhere...I think we might be outnumbered. The people who might be able to help may be *them* now. It happened too suddenly. I mean, they can't drive cars, so they wreck."

"They kill people. They attack them until they're dead." Cheyenne agreed, "Doesn't matter how old or young. They don't...they're not zombies. They don't eat them, but they'll bite them to kill them. Or tear them apart."

The infected woman snapped at Cheyenne's hand holding the door shut.

"It doesn't seem to be necessarily communicable," I said, "Not like a zombie virus. And people did seem to get the infection, like those who had the pink splotches but didn't turn, they passed on without becoming one of them."

Janessa nodded, knowing I meant her mom.

"Their only instinct seems to kill those who aren't infected," Cheyenne gripped the door harder as the woman pushed, making low groaning and clicking sounds.

Janessa was staring at the woman's overly wide, staring, diseased eyes.

"Are you going to be able to do it?" I asked Janessa.

She brought the Remington to her shoulder.

"Wait," I said.

They stared at me as I put my fingers in my ears and leaned back from the door.

"Seriously?" Cheyenne asked.

"Hey, I'm going deaf here with your shotgun and her rifle."

They gave each other amused looks and Janessa raised the rifle back to her shoulder.

Cheyenne held up her hand, "Count to three, let us get out of the way on three so the glass won't go all over him or me, then fire."

She nodded and began counting.

On the count of three, we turned away, just as I gave a slight push against the door to force the sick woman back slightly.

Fingers in ears are useless. Guns are *loud*.

The glass shattered, and the diseased woman fell backward.

Janessa massaged her shoulder, "That really hurts!"

We noticed she wasn't crying or upset as much this time as she slid back the bolt and ejected the spent shell. Not crying for shooting the person or her shoulder.

"You'll get used to it," Cheyenne said, pushing Janessa's rifle barrel toward the ground then entered the building with her weapon ready.

I drew my Colt and Janessa came in behind me.

We shot the already dead in the head, they weren't diseased, just unlucky. Better safe than sorry. One of them had a broken neck, the other harshly chewed. Two more people lay dead in the back, not diseased but unlucky, and the side door to the open garages was smeared with blood but when we looked out, no one wandered inside any of the bays. The door swung either way so we assumed they came in, killed, and went back out judging by the blood trails leading out the side of the open garage doors and leading off into the woods behind the business. We locked the garage bay door from inside in case a Roamer decided to try to come in from the garage and surprise us.

It took us twenty minutes to find the keys, then ten to find the right keys. We left the keys for the black van in its ignition so we could start it up as soon as we brought the survivors back. Janessa rode shotgun with me, armed with her Remington. Cheyenne led the way, her weapon and two boxes of shells lay in the Suburban's passenger seat since she knew the back roads better.

I would have to ask her how she knew them so well. This parking thing? Interesting and worthy of further study.

Cheyenne motioned for me to follow because we had to stop at a mom and pop gas station to fill up our gas tanks. Mom and pop were long gone along with the owners of a vehicle parked in the front. The closer we neared the main roads in the direction of the funeral home, the number of Roamers increased. They decreased the further out of town.

Once we neared more businesses oriented areas, we didn't hear any machine guns or roaring so we hurried toward home base, it appeared to be safe.

We didn't encounter any Runners or Volcanoes on the way but lots of dead, swarms of flies, and Roamers.

We pulled into the funeral home parking lot and faced the closed garage doors. I drove past Cheyenne and up to the front of the building, up onto the grass by the front windows and revved my engine because I didn't want to attract unwanted guests by blowing my horn.

One of the young girl's faces peered out between the drapes, I waved and she disappeared.

I backed up and aligned myself beside the Suburban as the garage doors rolled open to the left, preparing to receive us.

As the doors opened we smiled at each other as the Humvee's hood appeared aimed at us ready to leap back out into the fray. The others had made it back safely.

We stopped smiling when the left side of the Humvee came into view.

The middle section from the turret down into the cab was dented in by two feet.

Blood covered that side of the vehicle and Roger, shirtless, without his cap, his hair, chest, and beard soaking wet, waited for us with a hose in one hand washing the blood off the Humvee.

Chapter 16

There was only room for three vehicles in the garage, so Cheyenne parked on the far end from the Humvee and I parked in the middle.

Cheyenne jumped out of the Suburban and hurried around the front of the Jeep.

Roger put his cap back on by the time I opened my door and Janessa climbed out. The garage gate already rolling shut.

"What happened?" Cheyenne asked.

Roger shook his head, keeping his eyes to the ground, "We got caught on a side street. Some cars T-boned each other and we had to ram 'em. It slowed us down."

Janessa joined Cheyenne, "Is everybody okay? Jerry?"

Roger gave them a lopsided grin as he patted the indentation in the Humvee.

"The boy kept firing right into her face. Right. Into. Her. Face." He looked teary eyed for a second, "The Tank slammed down on us and…" tears swelled, "…and the boy…he…started shooting with his sidearm. He kept shootin'…till she…pulled him out of the turret." He wiped his nose with the back of his arm, "We pushed through the wreck and took off. Pete says…it was quick."

Cheyenne and Janessa held each other and Roger turned his back to us.

"Where's Pete?" I asked.

Roger kept his back to us, "He's inside. Said he needed a minute. Had to go to the head."

Cheyenne and Janessa circled Roger and hugged him, he returned the hug but stared at the ceiling.

I was at a loss for words.

Pete and the other two men inside cautiously opened the connecting garage door. When they saw us and there wasn't any danger, they joined us.

Pete's eyes were red but he kept up a stoic front. The men were sad too but they were more interested in the Suburban which gave them a lifeline to freedom. Once we all regained our composure, we went back inside to the younger group. The youngest cried and called for Jerry. The brothers sat together quietly. The older children were numb. Pete made bad jokes to try to loosen them up but it wasn't working.

Roger put his shirt back on, dried his hands, grabbed a road map on a side table, unfolded it and put it down on the main table.

"I see you got us transport. Any others?"

I nodded, "There's another, a black van sitting beside a white suburban, we left keys in the van's ignition, a few trucks, lots of Sedans. But for muscle? The SUV and van would be best for everyone."

Roger agreed, "We can make our way back to the dealership and grab the other. We've seen other SUV's but they've been all banged up, or occupied with the sick folk. We should be able to crowd everybody into the Suburban until we get to the dealership then we'll split 'em up."

"Then what?" Cheyenne asked.

Roger shrugged, "Savannah. A hospital. The reserve station?" he scratched at his long beard, "I'll take suggestions."

Cheyenne, Janessa and I exchanged glances, "Don't you think big cities, if they're infected, would be a bad place to go?" I said.

Pete nodded, "Yep. It would be. But all the people, the survivors, might be there too. The military, the police, anybody who could help or know what's going on."

"We don't have any communications or intel no matter what. We've got our eyes and ears and that's about it." Roger said, "I'm thinking we need to find as many people who ain't infected and get 'em together. Safety in numbers."

We couldn't deny that.

"We'll get another," Roger continued, "Load up on supplies, half of the young'uns in one SUV, the other half in the van." He indicated the two men, "One of you will drive each of 'em." He looked at Pete, "We'll run interference. If we get split up, go straight on 80 till you reach Patterson. On the edge of the city limits, there's a brick mini storage place on the left before you get into Patterson. If we get separated we'll all meet up there. Leave notes on the first storage unit you come to in case we're late," He looked at us, "You'll be our flanking support. You run the hell outta that Jeep."

I grinned, "She takes a beating."

He grinned back, "Ladies? You got any suggestions on where to go?"

Cheyenne and Janessa looked at each other, "Let's just not go too fast into Savannah, we don't know what might be waiting for us." Cheyenne said and Janessa agreed.

Roger saluted her, "Yes ma'am. Received and understood."

"Let's rest up for a bit," Pete said, "the heat's killing me out there and we need food and water to keep going," he motioned at the kids with his good arm, "Everybody refill your water bottles and power drinks from the sinks. We'll need all we got. You little ones, if you can, you go ahead and take a little nap while we're getting things ready."

"We need to set a guard up front of the building," Roger indicated the oldest girl, "You watch…"

I stopped him when I realized how haggard the young girl looked, "No, I'll watch. You get some rest. I'll watch the front."

Roger nodded and sent the girl off with the others, "Fine by me, but you'll need sleep too. You might be in shock and not know it. Hell, I'm in shock."

I grinned, "We all are, probably."

He rubbed his beard, "I need a drink. I'd like something strong but a power drink'll have to do," He left to find his thirst-quencher.

I headed to the front of the building and realized I had two tag-a-longs.

Cheyenne was right behind me and Janessa followed her.

"Um. Don't you two want to eat? Sleep? Get some water?"

Cheyenne cradled her 12-gauge, "Safety in numbers."

Janessa held up two bottles of water in each hand, "I did bring water. I can sleep anywhere."

They waited for a response from me but I didn't have one and then Cheyenne made a face and tipped her chin toward the front door.

I shrugged and lead them toward the front room.

***

Janessa fell asleep in seconds once she sat down in the large, soft, leather sofa. Cheyenne stood at the opposite side of the double doors at the front of the funeral home from me. She peeked through the drapes like I did, and we grinned at Janessa's soft snores. Roger came in and said we were going to rest for a longer period than we thought, the youngest kids were irritable and tired and needed to be relatively fresh for our escape plan and not so fussy. The two other men watched the back and side of the building, Pete was filling up the Humvee tank. After Roger left, Cheyenne and I continued our watch.

We spoke quietly so we wouldn't wake Janessa. After a few minutes, I noticed Cheyenne's head dipping and nodding and she stumbled once, nearly falling asleep on her feet. Denying her protests, I led her to another shorter couch, pried her shotgun from her, setting it on the floor within easy reach, and pushed her down and lifted her legs up onto the couch and made her stretch out.

"I'm not sleepy," she said through half closed eyes, "I just need to relax for a second."

I nodded, "Yeah, I know, it's been a long day. Just lie there for a minute."

She nodded.

She was asleep before I could even reposition myself by the window.

Running my fingers through my hair, feeling the stickiness of dried sweat on my scalp and cheek, I scrubbed furiously at my dry eyes to keep myself awake. I sniffed my armpits. Whew! Well…we all stank. My shirt was not the only sweat-stained and cold drying one in the room as I glanced over at my two female companions. The two of them had sweat rings on their shoulders, armpits, necks, and chests. Each crossed their arms because of the air-conditioned chilliness in their sleep until they rolled over onto their bellies.

I took a deep breath and centered myself.

Using meditation techniques, I ran kung fu and tai chi forms through my head to keep my mind active so I wouldn't doze off. The adrenaline of this morning and the past few hours was draining away.

Movement caught my attention out the window.

Two Roamers meandered through the parking lot.

They looked like a husband and wife taking a casual stroll. They were dressed in summer clothing, both were white, the man was bald, the lady had long, red, wavy hair. They were roughly in their thirties, covered in purple spots with soiled clothing but no blood stains. They walked across the front parking lot from left to right, and I drew the drape slightly wider to make sure they continued their course to wherever and away from the funeral home. Then I looked back the way they came as I released the drape.

A Roamer stared at me from between two close-set trees.

At least I thought he was staring at me.

No.

He *was* staring at me.

He looked like a teenager, maybe eighteen. Blonde, curly hair, slim, hunched slightly over. No shirt, baggy surfer-style shorts, dirty sneakers.

I stared back at him, but I didn't move the drape again. Maybe he just saw the motion and sort of locked onto it.

He stepped out from between the trees and advanced onto the pavement slowly.

Oh, yeah. He definitely has seen me.

I started to wake Cheyenne in case I had to open the door and shoot him when he did a curious thing.

Much like a dog when it hears a strange noise, he cocked his head from left to right.

The Roamers that we witnessed hadn't done that sort of movement before.

He hunched, or crouched, deliberately, flexing his hands.

What was wrong with his hands?

His fingers were longer, elongated like they had extra digits. He pressed them to the ground and leaned forward onto them. His head twisting slowly back and forth but his eyes remained on the window where I hid.

It was freakishly disturbing.

I decided it was better to be safe than sorry and whispered Cheyenne's name.

The Roamer's head twisted to the left like it heard me, then it bolted.

It sprang sideways like a rabbit caught facing down a fox and ran in the same direction as the couple.

It hadn't been a Roamer. It didn't run like a Runner. It was something new.

Something that seemed intelligent.

Cheyenne whispered in my ear and made me jump.

"What is it?" she whispered again.

I described what I had seen.

She moved to her post and searched the lot, she shook her head.

"Are you sure about what you saw?"

I frowned, "Yeah, I saw it."

She shrugged, "Maybe you're seeing things? Seeing more than what's there."

Giving her a bemused look, she held up her hand, "I just mean, you need some sleep too. Lay down. Get some rest. I'll stand watch and if he comes back, or anything comes, I'll wake everyone up."

I peeked out between the drape and window.

"Hey. You." She whispered, pointing at me, "Sleep. Now." She shook her thumb toward the sofa, "Go."

I gave her a resentful look.

"I have two younger brothers and babysat several younger cousins. Those looks don't work on me. Go. Now." She tapped the shotgun, "Don't make me use this."

I glared at her which made her grin watching me reluctantly move to the sofa.

Oh, wow, this is soft.

This is Heaven.

But I'm too worked up about how that teenager moved.

It wasn't like any of the others.

I won't be able to get any sleep.

Chapter 17

My choked snort woke me.

Drool dribbled down my chin.

"You talk in your sleep," Janessa said from the window as I wiped away my drool.

She leaned against the window frame, finishing a sandwich and a power drink. Her Remington lay on the floor at her feet. Her long braids were tied back with a strip of cloth. Her skin was shiny as if she just used a washcloth to wipe away the dried sweat.

I grinned, "Yeah, I've been told that," I searched the room but it was just us two, "What's going on?"

She pointed back toward the main rooms, "The little ones are starting to wake so they're eating now. Janessa went to check our gear and weapons, she took a quick nap when I woke up but she just left. She told me about the guy you saw, I haven't seen him."

"Yeah, he was pretty freaky." I wiped my eyes, "He seemed smart."

She licked her fingers, "You might want to hurry if you're going to eat, the food Pete made may be gone. They've loaded supplies already into the big SUV and the Jeep."

"You seem to be doing better."

She shrugged, "It'll hit me sooner or later that my family is gone. Berndale is dad's home, his family…his family didn't see eye to eye on a lot of stuff with me and my mom so I wasn't really close with my cousins. My grandparents, his parents, died when he was younger. I never met them. My mom was from Boston. I still have family there. We used to talk to them on the computer."

She seemed to want to talk, so I waited.

She sighed, "We planned on visiting them later this month during summer break but…" She shrugged once more, "Who knows if they're okay? As far as I know, I don't have a family anymore." She turned back to scan the parking lot.

"Well," I said, "Until then, I could do with a little sister. I'm the youngest and never had someone I could pick on. It sounds like it would be much more fun to give than receive."

She smiled, shook her head and looked out the window, "What about your family? Don't you want to go find them?"

I scratched my head telling her the short version of my family dynamics, "I figured, after we found some help, if we have some sort of communications, I could contact them. Maybe after we get everyone to Savannah or somewhere. I could, I guess. Nothing I can do about it now. So, I'm just playing it by ear."

"They sound nice."

I nodded, "Yeah, they are. I'm the dreamer in the family, with my writing aspirations. The least serious of the group."

She laughed, "Least serious? You seem to be the most responsible person I've met."

I laughed at her, "You just don't know me well enough yet."

She turned serious and looked back at me, "Thank you for stopping for me. And for rescuing Cheyenne too. I like her, she's cool."

I nodded, "My pleasure. And yeah, she is, I guess."

She smiled wider, "You may not want her too close when you talk in your sleep, she might hear."

I frowned, "What? Did I wake her up?"

She looked back out the window, "It's not how loud you were, more like, what you said."

That was confusing.

Before I could ask more, Cheyenne came walking down the hallway and turned the corner with two sandwiches in one hand, a power drink in the other, and her shotgun cradled under one arm. She offered the sandwiches and drink to me.

"I figured you would be up by now. Or I was going to wake you. Enjoy this, it's all that's left." She took her position by the window, "We should be leaving within the half hour. Roger's getting the kids ready."

She had washed off too and braided her hair tighter. She looked good in my green tank top.

"Sorry about waking you," I mumbled through a mouthful of food, "and whatever I said while I was asleep."

Cheyenne glanced at Janessa who smiled and kept her attention focused out the window.

"Um...don't worry about it," she looked back out the window grinning too, "I couldn't understand what you said anyway. Your accent is too heavy."

I coughed, "*My* accent?"

"Hey. I sound perfectly normal," she responded.

"Yeah, to *you*."

"*I* understood what he said." Janessa smiled.

Cheyenne gave her a wary, wide-eyed, glare.

Janessa ignored her.

Okay, now I'm curious. What did I say?

Roger whistled from the hallway to my right, "Is it all clear out that way? You all ready to go?"

Janessa leaned back so she could look down the hallway and gave him a thumb up, "All clear."

Roger strolled into the front room with us and pat the sofa armrest, nodding at me, "We're loading the kids up now. That thing is roomy! And the options." He shook his head, "Never coulda afforded one of them on my disability, but I love it. So, are you three gonna ride together or do ya wanna ride shotgun with the kids?"

We glanced at each other, but no one said anything.

Roger grinned, "Yeah, you three want to stick together." He leaned on the armrest, "So you three take the rear. The Suburban'll be in the middle and me and Pete will ride out front. The M60 wasn't damaged, but we don't got too much ammo for it left. Pete says he's taking that position."

"But...his arm?" Cheyenne asked.

He waved dismissively at her question, "He's been like that since the nineties, he gets on fine with it. He can shoot one handed. He can grip sorta with his other hand, not great, but he can." He took off his Steelers cap and ran his fingers through his hair before putting it back on, "The ol' sorry cuss won't listen to me. He's demanding to man the gun. Ol' coot."

Janessa and Cheyenne grinned.

"Anyways..." he took a deep breath and stretched his arms over his head, his shirt rising over his round belly, "...he's got his grenades. He's fussing about not gettin' a clear shot at that Tank." He dropped his arms, "He says he wants payback for Jerry."

I nodded and finished my drink and stretched, "I guess we're ready to go." I looked at the others and they nodded.

"Let's get to it then," Roger said with one last check out the window.

The kids, the teenagers, and the two men were packed in the Suburban. The two men in the front. The oldest teenagers rode in the back and were armed so they could shoot out the rear.

Pete waited in the turret, he saw Roger's disapproving stare and the worried looks on the two women ahead of me.

"Don't start, you ain't in my chain of command," he pointed at Roger.

Roger threw another dismissive hand at him, "I'm through arguing with your ol' cranky ass. You couldn't shoot the side of a barn with *two* good arms."

"I can shoot you if you keep going on about it," Pete countered, "You're a big enough target."

"Pfft. Did you even load that thing?" Roger asked, leading us around the front of the Humvee.

"Yeah, with your daddy's tears for having you." He grinned.

"That before or after he told your momma to drown you in the bath water?"

"Shut up, you old cheater."

Roger grinned, "Don't blame me for your lousy poker skills. I still want my money."

"You ought to be ashamed. Those cards were marked."

We loaded into the Jeep, Janessa in the back. And we all rolled down our windows so we could get last minute instructions if needed.

Roger huffed, "Yeah, marked with skill. Don't forget my money."

Pete nodded, "You'll get your money. Later. After."

Roger gave him another dismissive wave, "Always *later*. Always *after*. Pfft!"

He climbed in and shut the Humvee door.

Pete's position partially exposed him on the dented down side of the turret. He winked at Janessa and Cheyenne as they leaned forward to tell him to be careful. He shook his good hand in imitation of shooting the M60.

We looked to our left and waved at the survivors in the Suburban.

"Alright, like we planned," Roger said, "We'll crank up at the same time as I open the gate and we go. Us first, Taylor pull out behind, let the Suburban back out then you follow us back to the dealership. We good?" He gave a thumb up.

We did the same, followed by the other driver and kids.

He clicked the garage door opener and the gate started rolling back.

"Start 'em up!" He commanded.

Our engines roared to life.

The gate slid to the side and we started to roll up our windows as I turned on the air conditioner.

I heard Roger curse before my window was halfway up.

"What the hell is that?" he asked, looking out at the parking lot.

I rolled the window down and looked out into the parking lot to see what he was looking at.

The long-fingered changed teenager sat on his haunches across from the garage, leaning forward on those elongated fingers, his head tilting left and right as the gate opened.

Chapter 18

"That's the guy. That's the thing I saw," I told Roger as everyone turned around and looked out.

The teenager lowered himself as if he was going to charge, but he didn't move, just crouched lower. His head continued to tilt in that canine way.

"Well, do I shoot him?" Pete asked Roger.

"Hold on," I said, "Don't do that yet."

Roger looked at me, "What's up?"

"I don't think he's like the others, I think he's intelligent."

Roger roared the Humvee's engine.

The teenager crouched lower but remained where he was.

"You think I should run him over?" Roger asked.

I opened the Jeep door and started to step out. Cheyenne grabbed my arm.

"What are you doing?" she asked.

Hell, I don't know.

"I don't know, I'm…going to see if he understands me."

She let me go, "Are you crazy?" she opened her door and climbed out.

"You two, get back in the Jeep," Pete ordered, his voice low.

Raising my hands, I slowly walked toward the rear of the Jeep. The purple teenager raised his head slightly, then looked at the other side of the Jeep, his eyes closed to slits and he lowered his head again.

"Cheyenne?"

"Yeah?"

"Are you aiming your 12-gauge at him?"

"Duh. Of course, I am."

"Lower it please."

"What?"

"Lower it please."

"*What?*"

"You heard me."

"I did. I'm just making sure *you* heard what you said. Janessa?" she whispered.

A slim barrel slid out between the tinted unzipped back window beside me.

Janessa's voice was muffled, "I'm watching him."

The teenager's head tilted back and forth as we talked but his eyes never left Cheyenne.

I stepped to the edge of the garage, hands still raised, I glanced over at Cheyenne.

She still hadn't lowered her shotgun.

I made a face and dipped my head at her.

She made a face back.

I made another face.

So did she.

I started to say something, she huffed loudly and lowered the weapon.

"Don't worry, I can still get him," Pete whispered above and behind me.

"Me too," Janessa said.

When Cheyenne lowered her weapon, the purple mutated teenager relaxed minutely. When Pete whispered, he glanced up toward Pete, and when Janessa spoke his eyes shifted to the Jeep.

"He can hear us. That far away. He can hear us." I said.

Cheyenne mumbled, "Can he hear me say 'you come at us and I'm going to blow you in half?'"

The teenager glanced at her, squinted, tensed again and lowered closer to the pavement.

"Well, I think he did," Roger said out his window.

"Do you understand us?" I asked, raising my voice slightly.

His gaze shifted to me, then back at Cheyenne.

I looked around the Jeep and the Suburban's group waited silent and unmoving. From fear probably, the kids' expressions were terror filled.

The diseased teenager suddenly looked toward his right. He raised his head and upper body. Way too much like a dog for my tastes, he sank down and his attention returned to us.

"Do you know what's happened to you?" I asked, "Do you realize you've changed?"

The teenagers head tilted left and right, but his expression didn't alter.

"My God. It's like...like he's a dog. A dog boy." Cheyenne whispered.

He raised and listened into the distance again, which made Cheyenne and I look in the same direction. But we didn't hear or see anything. When his attention returned to us, he gave us lazy looks, half closed eyes and crab-stepped slightly to his left. He glanced once more toward the right, then sprang, running off like he did last time. Not as fast as a Runner, more graceful, practically springy, but fast. He didn't glance back.

I looked back at Roger.

Roger sucked a tooth, "Well, that was something," his eyes widened suddenly, looking over my right shoulder.

Cheyenne whacked me in the back of the head before I could turn around.

"Are you crazy?" she asked, "Are you stupid?"

I rubbed my head, "Ow, I told you he seemed intelligent."

"Yeah, like a dog! It was fast, it could have attacked you." She shoved me toward the driver's side, "Get in the Jeep." She stomped back around to her side, "Just get in the Jeep."

Roger leaned out his window and whispered, "You sure you two ain't datin'?"

Pete leaned down, "Seems like it, don't it?"

Roger slapped my back as I passed him, "Don't make a woman mad son, you'll regret it."

Pete chuckled, "Like you would know."

"Shut up, and I do know," he grinned.

Cheyenne was buckling up when I got in.

"Don't do that." She demanded.

"Okay."

"I mean it. Don't do that."

"Okay." I buckled up.

"I really mean it."

I nodded.

Janessa leaned forward, "Yeah, don't do that."

"*Okaaaay.*"

The Humvee pulled out, I backed up, the Suburban backed up and followed the Humvee. I followed the Suburban. The garage door slowly slid shut.

I looked in the rear-view mirror for the teenager but didn't see anything.

"Taylor? I mean it." Cheyenne repeated.

"Okay. All right. I won't." I glanced in the back and Janessa was wagging a finger at me.

Cheyenne nodded, "Fine. Catch up with them." We rolled up our windows to take advantage of the A/C.

God. I've had less demanding women in my life and I actually *did* date them.

Chapter 19

We raced after the Suburban following the Humvee, Roger's maniacal driving clearing the diseased away on both sides ahead of us and left crumpled in our path.

Several Volcanoes attempted ejecting most of their vomit onto the Suburban with the Jeep receiving a light spraying. The Roamers began to gather in the streets and Runners made a dash for us once or twice. Pete's accuracy with that one good arm he still possessed, reduced their numbers. Cheyenne did her fair share, much to the distress of my poor eardrums, with Janessa finishing a pursuer or two from our rear.

I decided to give up hope on ever hearing normally again.

Locked wheels rumbled ahead of the Suburban making me hit the brakes just before the Suburban's brake lights came on and skidded to a halt. Before I could decide what was happening, the backup lights brightened on the Suburban and the kids in the back started waving us back, screaming in horror.

I shifted to reverse, threw my arm over Cheyenne's seat backing up, as Janessa ducked and the Suburban roared backward toward us and we backed up away from it.

"Oh, shit. Taylor? Oh shit." Cheyenne muttered beside me as the M60 began chattering its rapid cadence.

I chanced a quick glance back at the Suburban.

Runners ran past and swarmed over the vehicle as children shrieked.

"Janessa! Clear our path! Find me somewhere to turn the Jeep around!" I ordered.

Cheyenne leaned out the window again, firing her shotgun.

The M60 chattered, the kids screamed, the Jeeps engine roared, grandpa's 12-gauge thundered, Janessa fired, Cheyenne yelled gibberish, and I kept looking for a turnaround spot.

"There! Taylor, there!" Janessa screamed pointing to an open parking space between two parked cars on the left behind us.

"I see it!" I tugged Cheyenne's leg, "Get in! Or we'll have them inside with us!"

She crawled back in, pumped the window up, held onto the door and the handle above the glove compartment as I whipped the rear of the Jeep toward our left.

The Suburban flew by us in reverse, one of the side windows was shattered and the oldest girl fought with a Runner trying to climb inside. The three brothers kicked and punched her attacker. One Runner rode on top like he was surfing, even wearing surfing shorts. Two women held onto the hood and punched ineffectually at the windshield at the shocked faces of the driver and passenger. Two Runners kept pace along either side of the Suburban, a semi-nude black woman in her bra and panties and a black man in a jogging suit on the side closest to us. Their splotched skin was rich with purple.

"That's my track coach," Janessa whispered in surprise.

On the other side, a blond male teenager in shorts and a redheaded woman with a black faux leather apron, covered in blood, flapped behind her as she ran.

"Oh my God, she used to cut my hair," Cheyenne said.

We looked back toward the approaching roar of the Humvee.

A small gathered squad of Runners pursued them, Pete switched to an assault rifle, maybe an AR-15, and fired with deadly accuracy. The Humvee wasn't moving at full speed, even though it was in reverse.

"He's giving the Suburban time to escape," I realized.

Cheyenne crawled between the front and back seats, grabbed her Winchester and aimed it out the side and began firing.

I leaned on the horn.

Pete looked over his shoulder, saw us, nodded, leaned into the Humvee's interior and came back out and continued firing.

I slammed the Jeep forward and we hurried after the others.

"Did he turn? Is he backing up?" I yelled, concentrating on the Runners in front of us.

"Yes! He's turning! He's turning around!" Janessa confirmed.

In my side mirror, the Humvee whipped into the space we vacated and pulled in behind us.

I swear Roger cackled madly the whole time, waving at me to hurry up.

The Suburban wiggled left and right, I assume to dislodge the outside passengers, Cheyenne shot the coach and the blond teenager, then the hair stylist and the semi-nude woman.

The Runner attempting to crawl into the Suburban's side window placing his feet against the vehicle and pulled the teenaged girl out the window with him.

They hit a parked car together, the young girl shuddered a few times but it was obvious her skull was flattened completely on her right side. The Runner staggered to his feet over her.

Cheyenne screamed, the Runner developed a third eye and fell as the Winchester cracked.

Janessa shot out the back window with the Ruger .22 through the zipper, "I can't hit anything! I can't hit anything!"

"Keep trying!" I yelled back.

The surfer dude on top of the Suburban realized we chased them. Cheyenne came back in for more shells just as the purple maniac launched himself directly at us.

"Look out!" I yelled, ducking and grabbing Cheyenne's head and shoving her down into the floor board.

The windshield cracked horizontally across its length as the purple diseased man's knees collided. He slid over the top and landed on the spare wheel. Janessa screamed in surprise as he grabbed her .22 barrel still extended out the back window. He jerked it out of her hands and tossed it behind us while finding a perch on the back tire.

His free hand plunged through the zippered opening and with one solid pull, ripped the plastic window partly free.

Janessa scrambled backward against the back of my seat, screaming. Cheyenne cursed as she hurried to reload the Winchester. Janessa suddenly appeared between the seats trying to climb into the front.

"Cheyenne!" I yelled, drawing my Buck knife and slapping it down on the dashboard.

She glanced up at me, at the knife, grabbed the knife, released a blood-curdling shriek and crawled over Janessa as I held onto the gearshift and pressed upward with my forearm so Janessa wouldn't throw us out of gear.

Blood sprayed over the passenger seat.

Cheyenne screamed, the Runner hissed and growled. It made loud clicking sounds. They struggled in the rear compartments confines, the back seat, and over the top of my camping gear and our supplies. Janessa attempted to load the Winchester but was so afraid she kept dropping the shells.

In the rearview mirror, it was utter chaos.

Arms and legs. Brown long hair and greasy, short brown hair alternated in my point of view. Blood. More blood. Bumping either front seats. The knife slashing back and forth. Up and down. Frustrated grunts and cursing. Was she biting him back?

Finally, Cheyenne rolled around onto her back and kicked the slashed, gored and bleeding Runner back out the rear window with both feet, screaming repeated obscenities about the sexual relationship between the Runner and his mother.

Janessa reached between the seats and retrieved a Glock just as Cheyenne finished five more loud sexual insults.

In my side mirror, I watched Roger aim at the tumbling Runner and run him over.

Cheyenne turned around and looked at me in the mirror.

With an extremely calm demeanor, she asked, "Hey? Have you got a first aid kit in your gear? I think I cut myself."

I thought she was joking until I glanced back and saw her unencumbered hand bleeding and several gashes on her arm and chest. A flap of skin over her left breast dampened her shirt. The Buck knife fell from her loose fingers.

"Cheyenne? Are you okay?" I demanded, "How bad? How bad!"

Her expression became confused as she pressed the bleeding flap of skin closed, blood leaking from the sides of the flap, "I…think…I'll be…" she glanced up and her eyes rolled up as she tilted forward, Janessa grabbing her head as she fell.

Janessa hastily brushed Cheyenne's hair out of her face and rolled her onto her back.

"Oh, God!" Janessa gasped, "Oh, God!"

"How bad?"

"I...I..." Janessa pressed her hands over Cheyenne's chest wound.

"Listen to me! Listen to me! In my duffle bag, on the end, in the side section, there's a first aid kit! Get it!"

"Okay. Okay." She said, climbing over Cheyenne.

The Suburban ahead of us found a place to do a three-point road turn and they turned around, throwing the unwanted passengers off the hood before returning to forward momentum. Through the shattered side window as they turned, we could see the kids screaming and crying.

Pete's AR-15 sang. In my side mirrors, the Runners still pursued us.

"Got it! I know what to do!" Janessa yelled, "I know what to do!"

I beeped at the driver ahead of us and pointed to a side street trying to get us back onto the back streets Cheyenne showed us on the way to the dealership.

"Do what you can!"

Janessa mumbled as she tore into the professional first aid kit, "I've got you, Cheyenne, I've got you. My mom showed me how to do this. You're gonna be alright. I'll make you better. Hang on," She repeated acronyms as she tore into bandages, and my attention returned to the Suburban.

Roamers bumped off the sides as they raced between streets. I rolled down my window to give hand directions to the Suburban driver and turned on my directional blinkers for emphasis. Occasionally blowing my horn to get his attention or the kids looking out the back. The kids in the rear gave verbal directions to the driver.

Pete's firing tempo slowed and finally ceased behind us. Through the flapping, tattered, back window, Pete leaned down and patted Roger on the shoulder as we bumped over the interconnecting streets, then he reloaded the M60 and returned to his position.

I honked at the Suburban to get their attention as we crossed a street I recognized as one street away from the back roads to the dealership and waved that they should turn right at the next intersection.

An oncoming blur, flashed in my right peripheral vision as we crossed the main street before going into the next side alley.

I had time enough to glance back into the rear mirror over Janessa's frantic ministrations to see the mutated Tank launch itself head first in a tackling posture directly into the Humvee behind us.

With a loud whump, followed by more, the Humvee and Tank disappeared from view.

Chapter 20

"What was that!" Janessa screamed.

I slowed the Jeep, the red Suburban continued forward and turned right.

"The Tank! Oh, Crap!" I stopped the Jeep, "The Tank!"

"Taylor?" Don't stop!" Janessa cried, "It'll kill us! You've gotta drive and Cheyenne's fainted. I'm trying to stop her bleeding! We can't fight back! We've gotta go!"

The Suburban was on the back road. There weren't many Roamers and no Runners around us.

"Taylor?" Janessa stared at me in the rearview mirror.

I put the Jeep in reverse.

"No! No! What are you doing? It'll kill us!"

"Jay, they lost Jerry. We've got to go back to see if they're okay. We can't leave them." I tried to remain calm as we hurried back to the intersection.

Janessa began praying as she ripped tape and gauze.

"Keep doing what you're doing."

She nodded and prayed as she worked.

I didn't look at Cheyenne, I took it on Janessa's word she had just fainted. It was expected with everything she'd been doing. My body shook with adrenaline as I drove.

We backed up to the middle of the intersection and looked down the road to the left.

The Tank lay face down several feet in front of the Humvee. Its legs shuddered slightly.

The Humvee lay on its left side, a huge dent in its right side. Liquid drained from the engine compartment and the wheels slowly turned.

There was no sign of Pete or Roger.

"Taylor. We have to go." Janessa begged, "Taylor?" she gripped my shoulder, "Taylor? We have to *go*."

I squeezed the steering wheel so hard I thought it would bend.

"Janessa, I...I can't leave them without knowing."

"Cheyenne," she begged, "Think about Cheyenne."

Damn it all to hell.

I put the Jeep in neutral, "I've got to see if they're okay."

"I can't drive a stick!" she said.

Damn it. Damn it. *Damn it*.

"I'm sorry. I couldn't…I wouldn't…leave you or Cheyenne if you were hurt. I have to go see."

That gave her pause, "Go. But come right back." She placed her bloodied hands together and prayed.

I jumped out of the Jeep, drew the Colt and ran toward the Humvee.

Roamers kept their distance further down the street. They weren't advancing and their attention appeared to be directed toward the Tank. I think they were afraid of it.

The Tank smelled horrible up close. The spikes rising out of her back and sides looked like solid bone. The purple splotches were as big as my hand. The large ugly protrusion the Tank called a head, bled from a deep gash. Up close, her face was even more distorted, her hair nonexistent. The dark, blackish, syrupy goo the diseased had as blood, was pooling around its shoulders, steaming on the hot pavement. The thing was still alive. I think it smashed the Humvee head on and knocked itself out.

Wiping the sweat from my forehead, either from tension or heat, and turning my back to the Humvee but carefully watching the Tank, I backed around to the opposite side.

It must have rolled a few times after she struck. Dents covered every angle of the chassis. Roger saw me through the shattered windshield as I came around the side of the Humvee. Missing his hat, he bled from his mouth and his forehead. He leaned up on his left elbow. I touched a finger to my lips to indicate he should be quiet. He scrubbed at his eyes and waved. I hurried around to the turret to check on Pete.

Pete lay crookedly inside. His neck was tilted at a weird angle, but he saw me and licked his lips. His Harley Davidson shirt was ripped and his arms lay at weird angles to his body. The M60 was gone.

"Hey, you missed one hell of a ride," he grinned as I came closer and shushed him.

"Whisper. The Tank knocked herself out. She's on the other side of you. How bad are you hurt?" I asked him.

"Ah hell," Pete laughed, "That was a roller coaster. Saw her at the last second and ducked. Can't feel anything below my neck. Got a feeling I'm completely paralyzed now."

Roger reached back and gripped his friend's shirt, "Yeah, a hell of a ride. Man, that was crazy. She tried that last time. Didn't see her," he gripped Pete's shoulder, "Sorry, bud."

"It is what it is. You probably need glasses. Shouldn't be driving anyway."

Roger laughed quietly and looked up at me when he noticed I was staring at Roger's lower half.

The dashboard pressed his legs impossibly flat and the steering wheel pressed deep against his Santa Claus belly.

"Roger-"

He waved at me, "Don't need to say it. I can make my own diagnosis. I can't feel nothin' below my waist. I think my legs are severed but I'm pinned so I ain't bleedin' out. How's everybody else?"

"We lost the oldest girl, but the rest are heading to the dealership. I…had to come back."

Pete coughed, "How are them pretty girls with you? That Cheyenne? She's badass."

"She cut herself while she was fighting that Runner and passed out. I don't think it's too bad. Janessa's taking care of her. Patching her up."

Roger glanced up at Pete and Pete grinned and they said together, "Milly's girl."

I grinned and lowered my voice, "Guys? I don't know what to do about you."

They exchanged another glance.

Roger sighed, "Ain't nothin' you can do. He's busted, I'm busted, I'm trapped. You gotta take care of them girls and the survivors. Get 'em to Savannah. Or just get 'em help somewhere."

Pete coughed, "Hey. At least take my Thumper. She's laying just inside the lip in front of me. She's got three shells left on the belt, and one already in the chamber."

I fished the launcher out of the inside of the turret and retrieved the attached belt, "I'm not sure how to fire it."

"There's my girl." he coughed seeing the launcher, this time, blood flecked his spittle, "Get back away from us and fire a few rounds. She's easy to operate. You have to angle the trajectory. Take that ugly Tank out. Can you figure out how to eject the shell?"

Playing with the launcher for a few seconds and a quick verbal lesson on how to use it, I was ready to fight back, at least I hoped.

I frowned trying to think of some way to take them with us, "I can't…"

Roger shook his head, "Pfft, you can. Ain't nothin' we got left. Get them all out of here Taylor. I'm the ranking man here and that's my orders."

I smiled, "I'm not military."

They chuckled, but Pete said, "Hell, nobody's perfect."

"You would have been a decent sailor." Roger winked.

Pete coughed, "Even better than that, a decent soldier."

"Now don't be cussin' the man."

"Shut up, you."

Roger nodded at me, "Really. Get out of here before she wakes up. Shoot them grenades. Aim for us first, though, we got a poker game to get to."

Pete chuckled, "If I die first, St. Peter'll know you're a cheater."

Roger laughed softly, "Like either of us will ever see St. Peter."

I tried to think of something to say.

"Go on, son," Roger said, giving me a small salute, "Our duties done."

"Time for you to take over," Pete agreed.

I gripped first one then the other on the shoulder and started to leave, hefting the launcher over my shoulder.

"Wait." Roger beckoned, "Wait, wait, wait."

I turned around.

"At least kiss that pretty girl. Please tell us you gonna kiss Cheyenne before we ship out."

Pete looked up at me, "Oh, yeah. You *got* to do that."

I smiled, "If she doesn't bust my jaw, I promise I'll *try*."

They laughed.

"Take care of Milly's girl too, ya hear?" Roger warned, "If'n she's anything like her mom, she's strong but got one hell of a big tender heart."

"Yeah, keep them safe."

I nodded.

"Get outta here now. You're making us all misty," Roger gave his dismissive wave.

I turned away and peeked around the edge of the Humvee. The Tank had shifted slightly but wasn't conscious yet.

I glanced up at the Jeep and softly crept by and around the monster, Janessa waved frantically for me to hurry up.

Picking up the pace several feet past the Tank's feet, I quick-stepped to the open drivers' side door and climbed in.

"Were they dead?" Janessa asked.

I lied, "They didn't last long." I examined the launcher, it loaded like a large barreled shotgun.

"Well, let's go," she implored.

"One last thing," I aimed the launcher at the front of the Humvee.

"What are you doing?"

I fired the first round.

BLOOP!

It fell short but exploded none the less. The Tank rolled over and extended her right leg in the air, the foot missing. She screamed. I ejected the shell, reloaded from the belt as quickly and as calmly as I dared.

BLOOP!

Aiming the next grenade higher, it struck the Humvee and the liquid running out of the undercarriage just as the Tank saw us and struggled to stand. The Humvee exploded into shrapnel. We ducked as debris flew toward us, chipping the sides of the Jeep. When the smoke and fire cleared, the Tank crawled toward us, minus its left arm. It was on fire from gas from the Humvee and its roars were deafening.

I angled the grenade launcher, loaded one more time with only one shell remaining.

BLOOP!

The grenade flew in between the concrete and cleavage of the crawling woman-thing before it exploded and flipped the monster backward onto the remains of the Humvee. The roaring stopping immediately.

"*Now* we can go." I dropped the launcher and the remaining shell in the passenger floor and shifted into first.

"Thank goodness!" Janessa said, returning her attention to Cheyenne.

I checked the main roads on either side this time before crossing over, "How's she doing?"

"Only one of the cuts was bad. I can do simple stitches. My mom taught me. The rest are just superficial. The one on her chest is deep, it'll need the stitches most but I can't do anything till we stop. I've cleaned it and have a compress on it and poured some liquid skin on it to temporarily stop the bleeding. You've got everything in your kit."

I nodded, "I like to be prepared. Remind me to never tell you what I was going to have my killer do with that kit in my story."

"Ew!" She made a face in the mirror, "I won't."

She grew silent for a moment, "I'm glad Pete and Roger didn't suffer."

I nodded, "I'm sure they're arguing over something right now knowing them."

She grinned, "Probably over the money Pete owes Roger."

"Yeah, probably so," I mumbled.

A roar rose behind us and we looked back toward the way we came as we made a right turn onto the back road to the dealership.

The roar wasn't energetic. Or angry. Or pursuing.

It was plaintive. As if it took all the energy the Tank could muster to roar its defiance against us.

"Could we go a little faster?" Janessa asked slapping the back of my seat.

"Oh, yeah, fast is good."

We hurried to join the others.
The roar died away as I shifted into fourth then fifth.

Chapter 21

A few Roamers scattered themselves on the pot-holed back road this time as opposed to the last time. They appeared to be wandering aimlessly, but who could tell? I noticed that some of them were beginning to shed their clothes or had them ripped off. Tufts of their hair were missing from males and females alike.

We pulled into the back gate of the dealership like we did earlier, the heat of the setting sun slowly relenting, but still cooking vehicles and pavement. It had been a long, long day.

We drove around in front, looking for the black van. Its space was empty. We looked for any messages from the other group on any of the adjoining cars but there was nothing.

"Park for now," Janessa said, "Give me a few minutes to stitch Cheyenne up."

Pulling the Jeep into the walking corridor between vehicles, I armed myself with the tactical pistol-gripped 12-gauge, made sure it was fully loaded and searched the lot for danger.

"Ow!" Cheyenne cried as I came around to the back of the Jeep to attempt to fix the back window.

"Oh, thank goodness," Janessa said, "Stay still."

I peeked in and Cheyenne's green shirt was pushed up and her double bras, the black and beige with front snaps she wore, were exposed, covered in drying blood. Her body shined with sweat and the bras were pulled slightly to the left so Janessa could work.

Janessa glanced at me just before I looked away, "Manners?"

"I'm fixing the window," I said with feigned indignation.

"What happened?" Cheyenne asked, trying to push herself up "What are you doing? Where are we?" she struggled, "Where are the others?"

Janessa hushed her, "Be still. I'm trying to give you stitches."

"Where's Taylor? Is he okay?"

"I'm back here," I said, "I'm fixing the window. Lay down and let Janessa work. Her mom taught her first aid."

"Ow!" Cheyenne said.

"Well, quit moving!" Janessa responded.

"It hurts!"

"Not as much as it would if you would quit moving."

"Where are we?"

I scanned the lot, "We're at the dealership. The others went ahead of us and took the van. As soon as Janessa sews you up we're going after them. *If* I can fix this window."

"So they're following the Humvee?"

Janessa and I exchanged a glance.

"What?" Cheyenne asked, "Oh, come on. Don't tell me something happened to them."

We told her what happened and what I did to the Tank.

Cheyenne didn't speak for a moment but I could hear her sniffing.

Janessa looked up at me, "Taylor, don't look in here, I have to unhook her bras."

I turned my back to the Jeep interior and kept inspecting our surroundings, "Tell me when."

Cheyenne hissed a few more times, a few more surprised exclamations concerning alcohol burning and then she was silent. "Okay, you can get dressed. It looks like it will stay now." Janessa said, "Don't itch it. Leave the bandage on. Your hand too. Pat them if they itch. I'm giving you these to take for the pain. If you need more, take more, but not more than the instructions say. You'll need food too."

A single Roamer moved along the road toward us but didn't look threatening. The Roamer wore only her white bra, brown with dirt. Her feet must have been frying on the hot asphalt but she didn't seem to care, her hair was lanky and ripped out too. Maybe they *were* fighting amongst themselves.

Janessa climbed out of the Jeep on the driver's side. She threw back her head and retied her long braids. Her outfit and knees were caked with dried blood. She reached back in as Cheyenne climbed out the other side and then she poured water on her chest, arms, and legs to wash the Runner's and Cheyenne's blood away.

Cheyenne whistled when she saw the back of the Jeep as she came around.

I noticed that even though she looked like hell, she was still pretty.

Sporting a four by four gauze pad with paper tape just below her left collar bone and above her breast, she softly patted the bandage and grimaced as she pressed the ones on her hand, thigh, and forearm. Blood spotted the pad. Her tanned face was pale, her thick braid a loose mess, and her clothes were sticky and smelly, drying blood covered every inch of her except where Janessa had sterilized with water or alcohol.

She handed me my knife, "Thank you."

Her eyes looked haunted, "Are you okay?" I asked, sheathing the knife.

She looked away and down, "Yeah, I'm fine, I hurt everywhere," she turned her back to me, "I'm just...I'm just..."

She crossed her arms and her shoulders began shaking.

Turning her around, she didn't resist as I hugged her.

Janessa climbed back into the Jeep and retrieved three bottles of water and two oranges, waiting as Cheyenne broke down. Janessa tried her best not to add to Cheyenne's tears. I set the tactical 12-gauge on top of the Jeep and pulled Janessa into our embrace.

We must have made a strange sight, the three of us standing in a deserted parking lot, releasing tension, all of us crying to one degree or another.

We calmed and Janessa shared the water and Cheyenne ate the oranges. I went back to trying to fix the back window. Opening the rear and shoving the partially bloodied personal belongings back into the small compartment, it looked as if the camping gear wasn't covered with too much blood and my backpack with my unused writing pads, notebooks, and my old laptop were hardly touched. I was an old-school writer. I start with handwritten notes, then put the story into the computer. Sadly, my laptop battery was dead, I hadn't used it in two days. Too much exploring around Hilton Head. The canned and boxed food that the survivors had shared with us was only slightly stained. The bag of money from *General Lee's* was untouched covered by the rest.

Janessa armed herself with her Glock and Cheyenne took the tactical 12-gauge from me as I tried my best to get the convertible's zipper realigned. Both drank and Janessa made sure Cheyenne ate another two oranges and drank a power drink. She also smacked Cheyenne's hands if she scratched at the gauze pads. Cheyenne would give her dirty looks but began furiously patting anyway.

Dripping sweat, I finally screamed at the torn plastic window in defeat.

"No good?" Cheyenne asked, wiping the back of her neck and patting her leg bandage.

Shaking my head, I leaned on the open door, "He ripped it all to hell. I can't fix it."

They waited for a solution. I pouted at the destruction on the exterior and interior and contemplated what a lack of a rear window meant for our safety and security not to mention a decent air-conditioned environment.

Cheyenne turned and shook her thumb toward the newer model Jeeps on the lot but didn't say anything. She raised an eyebrow.

I sighed, rubbing the top of my Jeep.

Janessa waited expectantly, sipping water.

Standing, I threw up my hands, "Fine. Let's go find the keys. But I'm not going to be the only one transferring our stuff into the new ride." I pouted, "Making me give up my loyal baby like this."

Cheyenne grinned and wrapped an arm around Janessa's shoulder as we went back into the dealership.

Looking back, my little two-door black Wrangler X sat worn, torn, battle-scarred, dented, scratched, dirt encrusted, blood covered, stank of human sweat and her interior held traces of monster blood and gore. Her windshield was cracked across its length, and a separate crack ran along the top. The black roof was a sickly gray from discoloration, and her paint was stained from Volcano vomit. Several small pieces of shrapnel were embedded on the side that faced the exploding Humvee. She had kept us alive on this incredibly hot, extremely bad, horrible day.

She still was my pride and joy.

Chapter 22

While I rummaged through the keys for all the Jeeps in the lot, Janessa and Cheyenne found clean T-shirts and hand sanitizer and took them to the ladies' room. I could hear Cheyenne hissing when the sanitizer stung her scrapes.

They kept the door propped open while my back was turned as Janessa helped clean Cheyenne's skin and her own.

Janessa smiled compassionately when Cheyenne walked out, patting her bandages. She wore a baggy gray T-shirt and she knotted it like she did mine earlier.

Janessa stood guard as Cheyenne and I searched and found a gas siphon in the garage, which we took out to the lot after making sure nothing waited for us.

We picked a Jeep Wrangler Rubicon, black of course, for our replacement.

Meh. My baby was prettier.

A four-door Rubicon with rugged off-road tires and four-wheel drive, a hard roof…bleh…with sunroof, and a front mounted winch which would probably come in handy. A new model, not pre-owned, or it at least looked new. An automatic, Janessa was happy about that, had a V6 engine and a steering wheel, finger-controlled, radio system. Not that there was anything to hear on the radio.

It had all the bells and whistles.

Pfft. More things to break and fail if you asked me.

I guess it was acceptable, in a pinch, if you like that sort of thing.

The back had more room than my Wrangler Sport. It also smelled clean.

Janessa pulled the Rubicon up alongside my old girl, parked and transferred the life blood from my loyal ride into the shiny replacement imposter so we wouldn't have to drive back to the mom and pop gas station.

Yes, our belongings fit better. Yes, it was roomier. Yes, it smelled better. Yes, it was easier to get in and out of. Yes, it was in better condition. Yes, the air conditioning was cooler.

Still.

I kissed my loyal girl's roof goodbye, ignoring the eye rolling from the others.

They just didn't understand.

We were able to examine passing Roamers from the safety of our new transportation as we sat in the lot before we went after the survivors.

Three nude men staggered down US80. Their purpled skin made them look like oddly upright lizards. They weren't wearing shoes, and like the female I saw when we first pulled in, they weren't concerned with the hot asphalt they trudged across.

"Why is their hair falling out?" Cheyenne asked, patting her chest bandage.

She was right. Their hair was patchy. I suggested that what I thought earlier was hair loss from a fight, maybe now was part of whatever they had contracted. Too many with missing hair was too much of a coincidence.

"Do you think they're still changing?" Janessa asked.

"It could be," The Roamers looked into the lot at our new Jeep, but they ignored us.

Cheyenne reached for her Winchester.

Stopping her, I pointed back at them, "Look. They're not coming toward us."

"Where are they going?" Cheyenne asked.

"Maybe they're just going in that direction, toward Savannah, until they find something?" Janessa suggested.

"Find what?" Cheyenne asked.

Janessa shrugged.

I put the Jeep in gear, "We'll worry about it later, we've got to catch up with the others."

We watched the Roamers as we pulled out. They watched us but they didn't react.

We headed toward Patterson City and Savannah.

Once back on US80, we encountered two Runners that Cheyenne and her scoped Winchester removed from our path. Roamers were spaced out along the road.

In cars we passed, the dead lay askew like something out of a Stephen King movie. Some diseased, trapped in their metallic oven coffins, banged at windows as we drove by.

The thermostat read one hundred and three degrees outside. The interior was a cool seventy-two. We appreciated the difference every time Cheyenne rolled the windows down.

The sun dipped lower but the temperature hadn't changed that much in the last week from daytime hours no matter where you lived. The heat was all encompassing.

We wove through parked and wrecked traffic. Sometimes going off-road. The Jeep was handy in that respect at least.

We contemplated what we and the other survivors would need if this was a country-wide outbreak.

"There's a super-store we could stop at in Patterson for supplies." Cheyenne offered.

Frowning, I shook my head, "Anything smaller? We need food, but supermarket superstores have large concentrations of people. More Roamers and Runners. What about a sporting goods store? One that sells freeze dried camping food? We also need to find the two of you some belts so you have something to attach your holsters to."

She nodded, "Yeah, there's an outdoor outfitter just off the highway. We could…"

Her left hand suddenly shot out and gripped my forearm.

She looked dismayed.

"What is it? What's wrong?" I asked, turning in the direction she looked.

The black van sat in a ditch on the side of the road, the doors wide open.

"Oh, no," I whispered.

"Maybe it's not them?" Janessa said, "Maybe it's just another van that looks like theirs?"

Cheyenne double checked her Winchester, "No it's them, look at the dealer tag on the bumper. Pull over."

"Pull over?" I asked, "Or slow down?"

Cheyenne didn't answer so I checked the surrounding area for Roamers, Runners, or dead which could be those Booby-traps. I pulled up behind the van and stopped. The changed people were spaced enough apart they didn't appear a threat. Legions upon legions of flies took flight as we drove by, dining on the dead.

Oddly only a few buzzards circled overhead. They were probably well-fed.

We got out. I had the tactical 12-gauge, Cheyenne had her Winchester and Janessa carried her Remington bolt-action.

Janessa kept her eye on our rear and flanks, Cheyenne moved to the right of the stopped vehicle and I moved to the left.

The van was empty. Of people, at least. The back still had a supply stash. Confounded, we circled around the vehicle to see if there were signs of a struggle or blood from a fight. We didn't find anything.

"Guys? The Roamers are getting closer," Janessa warned.

Cheyenne looked in the passenger side, "They left the keys."

I glanced in then Cheyenne crawled into the passenger seat, "Maybe the battery failed," I turned the ignition.

It started for a second then died, "I don't get it. Bad gas maybe?"

I looked at the control panel for signs of malfunction.

"You've got to be kidding me." I rested my head against the steering wheel.

"What?" Cheyenne asked, "What?"

They ran out of gas.

When I told Cheyenne, she smacked the dashboard several times with the palm of her hand.

"I told them! I told them where to get gas! I told them not to forget! I told them where the gas station was!"

"Maybe they couldn't get to it."

"They had time to transfer their supplies from one to the other. Time to get out here." She slid out and leaned against the open door.

We sat there silently for a moment.

"Guys?" Janessa said louder.

Behind us, Roamers increased their speed, but no Runners.

"There's nothing we can do. We can chew them out when we get to the mini storage."

She nodded with her eyes closed.

"Let's get back on the road," I suggested.

She nodded again and stepped to the rear of the van.

By the time I had stepped out of the van, Cheyenne had fired the Winchester twice.

I ducked and searched for danger.

Cheyenne marched back to the Jeep and climbed in, two Roamers fell behind the parked Jeep further down the road.

Janessa looked back at me.

"They ran out of gas. Let's go." I said as I stepped by her.

Janessa stopped me, "Taylor, I'm worried about her." She whispered, "She's starting to shut down. Emotionally. She's killing them too easily."

Cheyenne sat in the Jeep, loading her rifle, not looking at us, as I answered, "Yeah, I noticed. She's not doing so well. But none of us are. It'll be night soon and we'll get some better food in us, a good night's sleep, and start fresh in the morning. Just let her be right now."

Janessa nodded and we returned to the Jeep and the air conditioning.

Janessa bravely brought up her concerns nearly immediately to Cheyenne once we were moving again. At first, Cheyenne responded defensively, explaining her actions, but she admitted that maybe Janessa was right, then she asked me if I thought she was losing it. When I said she caused me concern, she admitted that she wasn't seeing the diseased as people anymore. She wanted her family back. She was angry and needed to do something about them. So, she lashed out.

We were still talking when we reached the wrecks blocking the road into Patterson.

Twenty cars or more and two Semis had smashed and shoved together and ran off the sides of the road and into the embankments pressed together like a warped three-dimensional jigsaw puzzle. Dead, pink-spotted bodies and gory unchanged bodies alike lay here and there. Roamers tried to crawl over the wrecks. Some Roamers were pinned between vehicles.

The red Suburban, filled with survivors previously, confirmed by its dealer tag, was smashed into the wrecks obstructing the road.

Chapter 23

Stopping the Jeep, we sat in shocked silence.

The Suburban's rear looked slightly ajar. The passenger's side door and shattered window faced us. No movement evident inside. The Roamers ignored it.

"Where are they?" Janessa asked.

We scanned the surrounding area. The Roamers shambled between vehicles. Some observing us, but none advancing toward us.

Cheyenne grabbed her grandfather's shotgun and made sure it was fully loaded. She shoved her Glock into the waistband of her cut-off shorts. I grabbed the tactical shotgun and Janessa readied her Remington.

"Let's go check," Cheyenne said.

"Keep watch, slow and steady," I made sure the Jeep could make an unobstructed hasty retreat if needed, "We don't want them to swarm us."

There appeared to be more than fifty, maybe sixty, Roamers wandering around the vicinity of the wreck pile.

"I'm leaving the Jeep running, don't shut your door all the way. It will make it easier to get back in."

They nodded.

Cheyenne looked back at Janessa, "Are you okay? Do you need to wait here?"

Janessa, while obviously frightened, shook her head, "No, I'll go with you. I'll be okay."

Cheyenne looked at me then back at her, "Okay, let's go."

We climbed out and headed swiftly and cautiously toward the red Suburban. The Roamers near us noticed us and strolled in our direction. Trapped Roamers began to make groaning, clicking, sounds.

That was new. Not so much the groaning, which made me think of zombies, but the clicking sounds. I noticed that the Runner Cheyenne fought with clicked too.

They were all losing their hair to various degrees. Whatever caused their illness was changing them fast. Looking around at the others nearby, some were nude, some even now shredding articles of clothing.

Cheyenne lead the way, then Janessa, then me.

Cheyenne made her way to the back of the Suburban, she pointed at the spilled supplies fallen and rolled beneath the vehicle. I nodded and she pulled the back open. More supplies fell out. Some were covered with blood. She aimed the shotgun in the interior and climbed partly inside. Her shoulders slumped and she slid back out.

She fought tears, "The two youngest are in there, they're dead. Torn apart. Nobody else."

Janessa moved to the passenger side and opened the door to check the front as I walked around to watch over them and the dangerously close Roamers.

Janessa backed out, "There's blood everywhere in the front."

Cheyenne moved around to the driver's side inspecting the ground.

Janessa stepped backward, swatting at flies from the passenger side and backed up against a wrecked car to the right of the Suburban.

She kept her voice low, "It looks like they rammed the wrecks. Why? Why would they do that?"

Before I could respond, a hand shot out of the car behind Janessa and grabbed her long braids and pulled her head back and down toward its owner.

"Janessa!" I shouted, as she slid on the road and bent further backward.

She screamed and dropped her weapon, reaching for her hair. I ran forward to shoot the creature inside. My yell and her scream caught further interest from the Roamers. The trapped ones increased their struggles and their volume of clicking and hissing.

"Get me out!"

The voice came from inside the car.

Janessa struggled with a withered set of claws tangled within her braids.

"Get me out! Get me out!" a shrunken elderly woman croaked.

"Let her go!" I ordered, setting my weapon on the hot roof of her car, it slid off and fell to the ground.

The old woman, with wild nasty hair, wearing smudged, sweat-smeared, heavy makeup, sporting dark coffee-stained teeth and a madwoman's bulging eyes, sat pinned in her seat much like Roger had been earlier in the Humvee. Her car was pinned beneath the tractor trailer body in front of her. Scattered around her lay three empty bottles of water, candy wrappings, crackers and empty cigarette packs.

"Let her go I said!"

Cheyenne came crawling over the crushed front of the Suburban her shotgun aiming at the car and moving from struggling Roamer to struggling Roamer.

"What's going on?" she demanded.

"You're hurting me!" Janessa cried.

"Get me out! Now!" The old woman hurled her words at us, "You get me out right *now*!"

I grabbed the woman hands. Her hold was astonishingly strong. She might have been old, but her muscles were backed up by the frenzied panic of a trapped animal.

"You better goddamn get me out of here right *now*!" she shrieked.

She pulled Janessa back and through the car window in her madness.

BOOM!

Cheyenne reacted to a Roamer who came too close.

"Taylor get her out of there!" Cheyenne cried, leaping onto the mangled hood of the old woman's car.

Janessa fought against her attacker, but the woman's fingers had dug deep and she even wrapped her wrists around Janessa's long braids.

"You get me the hell out of here now!"

"Let her go and we will!" I commanded.

BOOM!

BOOM!

"Let me *go*!" Janessa bent backward over the sill of the window, her right arm holding her hair and her left pressed against the hot window's top edge.

"You get me out of here!" the woman screamed, her dry voice cracking.

BOOM!

"Taylor! Shoot her!" Cheyenne screamed, "Shoot her!"

She surprised me with her order.

BOOM!

I glanced up over the roof and Roamers staggered faster toward us, Cheyenne fired toward the left and right.

BOOM!

"Let me go!" Janessa screamed.

I punched the woman in the face through the window, but it hardly fazed her.

"Get me *out*! Get me *out*!"

Janessa grabbed my belt to hold herself steady.

"Taylor!" Cheyenne screamed.

BANG!

Janessa tugged at my belt as I punched the old woman hard enough to bust her lip.

"Out! Get me out! Get me out now! You *whore*! You get me out!"

Janessa bumped my arm with her elbow.

I glanced down, she had drawn my buck knife and sawed desperately at her braids close to her head.

BANG!

Cheyenne was firing her Glock.

"Get me out! You get me out now! Now! You whores! You black whores!" the woman screamed.

Janessa cut once more then she wrenched her head free and away from the window.

"Ahhh!" the woman screamed, "*Ahhh*! Get me *out*!"

The old woman tried to untangle Janessa's cut braids from her fingers but she had twisted them too tightly.

"Back to the Jeep!" Cheyenne screamed, jumping down to the ground, shoving her shotgun into Janessa's arms and picking up Janessa's fallen Remington.

I grabbed the tactical shotgun laying at my feet.

"Get me out! You black whores! You black *whores*!" the woman continued screaming, "Get me out now! *Now*!"

Cheyenne fired the Remington at the advancing horde.

Janessa handed me my buck knife and I sheathed it, firing one handed to help Cheyenne repulse the creatures. Janessa ran past me toward the Jeep. The crazy woman in her car on one side of us and the abandoned red Suburban on the other.

Out of the corner of my eye, coming around the back of the Suburban on my right, a purpled hand grabbed my right shoulder.

Out of instinct and from many years of practice, I dropped my shotgun, grabbed the extended arm, pulled the diseased person closer and hip-tossed him over my right side and onto his back.

Cheyenne shot the purple nude and hairless man in the head as he tried to grab my leg.

Another changed female came around the back and I side-kicked her in the gut, shoving her back into the two lumbering young children behind her. All three of the diseased were nude and dirty. She fell back and landed on top of them.

Cheyenne shoved the tactical shotgun back into my hands and directed me toward the Jeep.

Backing toward the Jeep, we emptied our weapons into the rushing diseased attackers. Many of our shots went wild. Cheyenne was more accurate.

Janessa stood on the side of the Jeep in the doorway and fired her Glock over our heads. I doubted she hit anyone until a changed man clutched his chest and fell backward.

The screaming old woman had called to monsters and they responded, clawing at her through the window, but she kept screaming for them to get her out. Get her out right *now*.

Her screams stopped by the time I climbed into the driver's seat.

We shut our doors and the Roamers surrounded us. Shifting into reverse, I backed up.

"Taylor! There!" Cheyenne pointed as she and Janessa reloaded.

She indicated a steep incline on the left side of the road, the setting sun casting shadows against the ridge. The incline was free of vehicles and creatures.

I put the Jeep into four-wheel drive, shifting it into a lower gear and took off.

The changed bumped off the sides of the Jeep, or fell beneath us, as we roared toward our opening.

The tires dug in and we climbed. Pure adrenaline kicked in, and I drove like Roger as we rounded the low hill and drove around the piles of wrecked cars.

More Roamers waited on this side.

Hundreds.

Ahead of us were the smoldering remains of a crashed plane to the right of the road laying in a field obscured by the car and semi-truck on the other side of the road by trees just past the wreck pile. I supposed the pilot had remained human judging by the cleared path stretching along the road in front of us and the broken tree line and fallen trees. It appeared as if the pilot had semi-successfully tried to land the plane on the road. The wings were partially torn from the main fuselage, and branches stuck out of the cracked body. We could see where the plane veered off the road and lost its front wheel and plowed into pasture land before finally coming to a stop. The plane shoved all the cars ahead of it into the pileup and off the sides of the road.

I cursed as I veered left to avoid two Volcanoes. Ten Runners, standing near or beside the plane's remains, turned toward us and began pursuit.

"Reload!" Cheyenne grabbed my tactical shotgun and snatched more shells from behind the seat.

"On it!" Janessa yelled, reloading the Glocks.

"Get the Remington too," she added.

Obstacles lined the road, I kept the Jeep on the left-hand shoulder often riding up the incline. The Runners aimed toward us. I thought I even saw a small Tank watching us from the front of the plane but it didn't seem to have an interest in us. I decided not to tell the others we might have another Tank problem. It might have just been a big, tall infected person.

An open field broke the uniformity of the trees on my left and I turned off the road, leaping a small, deep, embankment. My passengers bounced in their seats and screamed, open boxes of shells scattered their cartridges in the floorboards.

"Trying to do something here!" Cheyenne cried, "Watch your driving!"

It must have been the adrenaline because she made me laugh.

The trees opened into a pasture of rolling hills in front of us. It looked like my grandfather's farm back in North Carolina.

"They're still coming," Janessa said.

In the side mirror, the Runners were leaping over the embankment.

I angled the Jeep toward a barb-wired pasture's fenced gate. I increased speed. Thankfully the fence was wooden and not steel like my grandfather preferred.

"Hang on!" I cried.

We smashed through the gates. To our right, startled cattle dashed off into the trees. They left behind dead calves where they lay and one or two cows probably dead from the heat and thirst.

"Are they still coming?" I asked.

Janessa paused, "Yes, they saw where we came through."

We angled around a hill and avoided a dry stream bed of hard-packed clay. It looked like the daily heat made short work of the only water supply for the cattle. I followed alongside the dry vein.

A thought occurred to me, "Janessa, are they bunched up? In a group?"

I could see the haphazardly cut remains of her braids in the rearview mirror as she looked back.

"Two are ahead of the others, about five...six...are grouped together. Why?"

"Cheyenne, do you think you can pick them off from here if I stop the Jeep?"

"Of course," she sounded insulted, "But I'll need some time to aim."

"You take the Remington, I'll take the Winchester. I'm heading for that hill," I pointed at a low rise in a long stretch of flat land, "When I stop, we get out and open fire."

"Can't we just outrun them?" Janessa asked.

I shook my head, "I don't know if we'll come to a dead end and have to double back. I don't want to give them help. You use grandpa's shotgun if they get too close."

She nodded and switched weapons with Cheyenne.

Another thought occurred to me, "Janessa, give me the grenade launcher, it's on the left side behind you."

I had reloaded the last shell when we transferred supplies to the Rubicon from the Wrangler.

She rummaged until she found it and handed it to Cheyenne.

We drove up the hill and I stopped the Jeep. We hurried around to the back, Janessa carried a box of shells for each of our rifles.

The purple, naked, diseased ran through the knee-high grass toward us. Insects filled the air from our passing and dry grass floated to the skies as dust settled around us.

Cheyenne knelt beside me in a shooters crouch. She dropped the grenade launcher between us.

"Before we start, sorry about your ears," Cheyenne yelled at me, sighting down her scope.

"What?" I asked.

"I said sorry about your ears!" she repeated.

"*What?*" I repeated, cupping my hand to my ear.

They returned my grin.

Cheyenne opened fire.

The fastest Runner staggered and fell.

The Remington click-clacked and she fired again.

She missed as I fired.

I missed.

She hit the next one, missed the next two shots.

We alternated shots, reloading as necessary.

It seemed forever before the clumped group were in the pasture's long straight path. More Runners had joined the initial group. They continued clumping together making it easier for us to take them down. I told Cheyenne to hold her fire.

I set the Winchester down, aimed Pete's launcher and fired the last shell.

BLOOP!

A moment later the grenade exploded.

Three of the Runners stumbled to stops and fell, one cartwheeled through the air.

As the smoke and dirt cleared, two Runners ran at a wobbly trot toward us.

Cheyenne fired twice. Two Runners fell.

We waited for the dust to clear and reloaded.

We waited some more.

We scanned the surrounding trees, the field, in the direction of the plane crash. We listened. We heard only the dull moan of the Jeep engine behind us.

Bugs harassed us. The sun dipped lower. We waited.

Cheyenne stood and stretched, perspiration soaking her body as she smacked furiously at her itchy, sweaty bandages. Janessa shoved her hands away and checked the wounds. I stretched and watched the fields for movement.

Janessa confirmed Cheyenne had only popped a few stitches but they remained together.

We drank some water and waited. The sun setting further.

"Let's go," I finally said, and we climbed wordlessly into the Jeep.

We were lost. Not in location, but in purpose. The survivors were gone. For the moment, our only avenue toward help was blocked by multiple afflicted people.

We went deeper into the pasture. We drove in circles just in case more Runners, or Roamers decided to follow our tracks and the Runners that we killed.

We came to another fence. This one Cheyenne got out and opened. Shutting it behind us.

We drove deeper and found an open area with several large ancient, leafy, dry, shade trees.

We pulled beneath them.

The sky overhead showed no clouds, clear skies, and gave us waves of heat even with the setting sun.

We climbed out and scanned the area, I turned off the engine and we listened but only perceived natural sounds surrounding us.

"Let's make camp," I said.

They were exhausted, I was tired, and there were no complaints.

My dome tent went up easily. I spread a tarp on the ground, pulled the winch line out and wrapped it around a thin tree and lay another tarp over it and secured the ends to trees for more shade over the tent. It was a six-person tent and I had an inflatable queen size air mattress I blew up with an attachment connected to the Jeep's lighter. We spread a blanket on the ground, I cooked us a hot meal with my small camp cooker, and we washed off with camping towels and bottled water. They marveled at the camping gear I possessed. Always be prepared was a great camping motto.

Janessa changed Cheyenne's bandages as I listened for monsters.

The sun had nearly set and Janessa stretched out my sleeping bag on top of the air mattress.

The temperature had to be no less than ninety.

We avoided speaking about the others we lost.

I gave them waterless shampoos and we washed our hair. Cheyenne trimmed the rest of Janessa's braids. She seemed to be resigned to losing her hair, she wasn't happy about it but she was alive. She laughed at herself in a small hand mirror I gave her. Cheyenne told her she wasn't good at styling but Janessa told her it was alright.

We decided ahead of time no fires. I used a crank emergency light with a radio. We gave it a full charge and tuned through every station. Only static. We kept the light off.

They sat on the blanket outside the tent, I sat on the bumper of the Jeep.

"Do you think any of the others lived?" Janessa eventually asking what we feared to mention, running her fingers over her hair.

"I say we assume the best," I shrugged.

"I meant to tell you," Cheyenne smiled, "I thought you were joking about knowing kung fu. Those were some pretty cool moves you did back at the wreck."

"He did kung fu?" Janessa asked, "I missed it?"

I gave them a swarthy look, "Yes, I *am* impressive indeed."

They grinned and Cheyenne said, "Yeah, well I said it was cool. Not impressive."

The sun set and we sat in darkness now.

"Can you teach us?" Janessa asked.

Cheyenne chuckled, "Yeah, now *that* would be impressive."

"I can and I will. As long as Cheyenne teaches us how to shoot better."

Janessa agreed, "Yes, please."

"I guess I can," she said to Janessa, "At least you're not scared of shooting now."

"I'm still scared. I'm not crazy about killing people. Even sick ones. But it's what we have to do. I don't want to die."

"You did good today. Both of you," I said.

"Yeah, not so bad yourself," Cheyenne said.

I leaned back against the Jeep, got burned on the still hot metal, and leaned forward again.

Janessa stretched her arms over her head, "Well, I think I'm going to turn in. I think that mattress will feel great about now."

"Any plans for tomorrow?" Cheyenne asked me.

I shrugged, "Gear shopping. Look for survivors. Live."

"Sounds good to me," Janessa crawled into the tent, "Night everyone."

Seconds later, she prayed.

Cheyenne stood and stretched and joined me by the Jeep.

"We tried to save them," she said quietly.

"We did. And they may have survived. We didn't find bodies."

"C'mon. You saw that crowd. That's between us and Patterson. We didn't meet the survivors coming back toward us. They're gone," she sighed, "but we tried our best."

"Yeah," I stretched, "You better go to sleep. I'll stand watch."

Her head tilted sideways, "No, huh-uh, you need sleep too."

"I'll stay up for a while," I popped my back, "You go ahead, I'll be fine."

Janessa's soft snores drifted through the open mesh windows of the tent.

She could fall asleep faster than anyone I ever met.

In the darkness, Cheyenne took my hand, "Taylor. You need sleep too."

"I'm good. You go ahead."

"Taylor. You look terrible."

I laughed, "Gee, thanks."

"No, I mean it. You've got circles under your eyes. You nodded off several times while we ate. You've nearly fallen forward twice sitting here."

Do I? Did I?

"You don't need to stand watch. We're okay here," She tugged on my hand, "Come get some sleep before these mosquitos drain you dry."

I stood and it took effort. Maybe she was right.

"That's better."

"Do you believe in keeping promises?" I asked.

She let my hand go, "I do. Why? You need me to make you promise to go to sleep?" she smiled in the darkness.

"Roger and Pete made me make them a promise."

"Oh, yeah? What about?"

I leaned forward and kissed her on the cheek.

She leaned back, one eyebrow lifted higher "They made you promise to kiss my cheek?"

I squirmed, "Yeah, more or less."

"Uh huh," she said, "Boys. No matter the age."

She suddenly took my face in her hands and kissed me, firmly, gently, without parting her lips.

I was stunned, her lips were incredibly soft, full, and warm.

She leaned back and let me go, "I really think that's more along the lines of what they meant."

She turned and knelt toward the tent front flap, "Coming?"

"I…uh…can sleep in the Jeep."

"Yeah, you can. But you're not going to," she extended her hand in the darkness, "Come on."

I took her hand and crawled inside, we set our weapons inside the front flap.

Janessa mumbled in her sleep and rolled over. She lay on the right side of the tent, Cheyenne crawled to the left and motioned for me to get in the middle. I zipped the tent closed. We were tightly packed but had enough room to move.

As I lay down, she leaned over and whispered to me.

"Thank you."

I whispered back, "What for?"

She smiled, paused, and whispered, "Go to sleep."

I shrugged, laid back and tried.

During the night, before I did fall asleep, they jolted in their sleep and lurched awake multiple times apiece. I alternated calming them and convincing them in their twilight half awakenings to go back to sleep. Telling them they were safe, nothing was going to harm them.

The twitching and sudden awakenings happened many more times before they relaxed into a reasonably restful sleep.

We had survived the first day of the change.

As I lay there, attempting and failing to ignore the heat and humidity, listening to any changes in the sounds of the night warning us of danger, and staring at the stars through the tent window, one thought continued in my head as I drifted off to sleep.

What *would* tomorrow bring to the unchanged?

ABOUT THE AUTHOR

When not practicing or teaching Kung Fu, T. M. is reading or watching horror, thrillers, or sci-fi movies.

B-movies? The cheesier the better. Classics? The butler did it. But it was his twin taking his place you saw for two minutes, in shadows, at the beginning with the pair of scissors shown for two seconds in the middle of the movie. See?

T. M. prefers writing in the horror, science fiction, post-apocalyptic and, occasionally, romance genre.

T. M.'s favorite authors include Clive Barker, Patricia Briggs, Dean Koontz, and Edgar Rice Burroughs.

Novels by T. M. Starnes

Crazee Teena

The Unchanged

The Unchanged Survivors

The Unchanged Safe Harbor (Coming soon)

Anthology short story selections by T. M. Starnes

The Appalachian Terror Trail: The Path is paved with fear Collected by Tamara Woods

Enter the Apocalypse Edited by Thomas Gondolfi

Made in the USA
Columbia, SC
25 April 2024